Head of the Serpent

by Allen Manning & Brian Manning
Cover by Allen Manning

Copyright © 2018 Allen Manning

CHAPTER

1

Eight months have passed since the United States government decommissioned the Hostile Response Division. Under the supervision of the US military and critical personnel in the Department of Homeland Security, the HRD was a joint task force, responsible for combatting domestic threats with international ramifications.

Pryce Windham was one such man, attempting to acquire a prototype weapon, capable of defeating the most sophisticated encryption, to engage in cyber warfare. Pryce was on the verge of shifting the balance of power in the global theater of war, selling his *talents* to the highest bidder.

Recruited by the HRD at that time, John Stone lent his talents to the team to track down and stop Windham. For John, it went beyond the mission. He had a personal stake in the matter, tracking down the men responsible for murdering his friend, Frank Colt, and kidnapping his goddaughter, Emily.

During that time, John found himself accused of committing acts of domestic terrorism. The Secretary of Defense relieved Marvin Van Pierce, the Director of the Hostile Response Division, of command. The Hostile Response Division took on a new mission: find and capture John Stone.

On the run, and hunted by two opposing forces, John eventually stopped Pryce Windham, revealing evidence that linked him to specific government officials in direct command of the HRD. With the help of his friends still in the HRD, it was more than enough to clear John of all charges.

DHS spearheaded an investigation to uncover the depths of corruption within the government. The aim was to identify and remove the people responsible for infiltrating the Hostile Response Division, and any other branches and organizations compromised by the treasonous acts.

John felt the investigation would be fruitless, with corrupt influence still holding sway over crucial positions of power conducting the investigation. It would be years before the cancer could be rooted out, and he no longer had the desire to work for the Hostile Response Division, or any organization similar. John stepped away and returned home to his previous his life of peace.

* * *

Great Falls, Montana

The sun rose through the clear blue sky, radiating its early afternoon heat. A late spring breeze blew defiantly against the arrival of the coming summer. John Stone wiped an arm across his forehead as he stood to admire the repairs he made to his porch railing. He found himself away from his home for much of the past year, but now that he was free, he spent his days fixing the place up.

The hammer clanged into his toolbox as John dropped it before flipping the lid closed with his boot. He hoisted the tools up as he looked off in the distance. The sound of a car approaching reached him before he could actually see it. A dark sedan drove past the surrounding trees into the clearing and pulled up the long dirt road to his estate. It was no surprise to John, as he lived in a somewhat secluded area, and any car around here would be heading to his house.

The car slowed to a stop on the driveway, tires crunching along the gravel, and the driver side door swung open. A fit man with a light brown complexion

6

stepped out. He kept his hair cut short, but was currently sporting the stubble of a beard that was only now starting to show a little gray. His easy-going expression was a contradiction to the authority he could exude with little effort. The man smiled, revealing a set of straight white teeth, set into a square jaw.

"It's been a while, huh John?" he said.

"Not long enough to have to see your ugly mug again," John said.

Marvin Van Pierce gave him a look of mock offense.

"Son, if you were half as good-looking as me, you would shave that mustache off so everyone could see your face."

After a moment of intense stares, both men erupted into laughter.

"Come on in. I've got some beers in the fridge," John said, as he gestured to invite the man into his home.

* * *

The interior of John's mountain cabin was sparsely decorated, yet comfortable. Though not minimalist, everything inside had its purpose and was sturdy in design. Its utilitarian nature reminded Van

Pierce of the precision of a military barracks but done with warm wood colors and plenty of natural light from the cabin's windows.

John led Van Pierce to a small, round oak kitchen table. Marvin took a seat, and John pulled two bottles of beer from the fridge. He twisted the tops off and slid one across the table as he sat down. Marvin took a long swallow of the ice cold drink and let out a sigh. The two men sat at the table like they were about to share stories of *the good old days*, but both of them knew that's not why the former **HRD** Director would have driven all this way to visit.

"Any progress on the investigation?" John asked.

"You don't waste time, do you, John? Always a straight shooter," Van Pierce said.

John took a sip of his beer but said nothing.

"As a matter of fact, the investigation is still ongoing. The reports say they found one or two people involved in the lower level government positions. They have yet to find any evidence implicating any officials at a higher level."

"Why am I not surprised?" John asked.

"Hey, there's nothing we can do about that right now. Let's be thankful that you were found not guilty of any wrongdoing, and just move on."

Marvin took another sip from his bottle. "Besides, that's actually not why I'm here."

John raised an eyebrow, curious.

"I'm consulting," Van Pierce said. "I help other people catch bad guys now. Got a job working with a counterterror task force in France."

John nodded, twirling a bottle cap between his fingers "Sounds lucrative."

"It pays the bills. If you want to come with me, I can make a call—"

"No. I'm done," John interrupted.

Marvin's expression didn't change. He knew John would refuse.

"Figured you wouldn't be interested, but I needed to toss the offer out there anyway. If you ever change your mind, just say the word and you're in," Van Pierce said.

John didn't speak, instead lifting his bottle and tilting his head in a *thanks for the offer* gesture. He was really settling into this quiet, peaceful part of his life right now.

They finished the rest of their beers, admiring the serene view out the window and sharing some casual talk to catch up. John stood up as Marvin prepared to leave.

"It's been nice seeing you again, *old man,*" John said with a grin.

Marvin laughed and clapped him on the shoulder. They shared a firm handshake between two tough old soldiers.

"Goodbye John."

"Goodbye, Marvin." John watched the man head out the door. He was not as tall as Stone, but Van Pierce projected an authority that many were not capable of.

John stood on the porch giving one last wave as the dark sedan pulled away, and back down the dirt road. He contemplated the offer, tempted to feel that rush again, but the feeling left as fast as it came.

The quiet life was all he wanted now. John finally turned and walked back into his house.

CHAPTER

2

Lyon, France

Three days after his meeting with John Stone, Marvin Van Pierce was in France, coordinating with the elite tactical unit of the French National Police. Known as RAID, the *Recherche, Assistance, Intervention, Dissuasion* unit was responsible for counter-terrorism operations within the major cities of the country.

With the recent deactivation of the Hostile Response Division and the reassignment of its active military members, Van Pierce became a highly recommended consultant, by close contacts that he maintained with the United States government. His knowledge and experience battling terrorist groups and investigating acts of terrorism over the past 40 years made him a formidable asset.

On his current assignment, Van Pierce lent his knowledge and experience to the French government, coordinating with them to help locate and stop a new terrorist group that had splintered from ISIS. Though the group went active less than one year ago, they've already claimed responsibility for three public terrorist attacks throughout Europe, the last one occurring only a week ago. Now, Van Pierce sat in a small meeting room with Maurice Ouvrard, the General Secretary for Administration in the Ministry of the Armed Forces, Lionel Gavreau, the RAID task force leader, and his second-in-command, Christopher Brassard. A computer analyst and a language translator also sat in the room, to help out when needed.

Various photos plastered one wall of the room. Shots of French landmarks and government buildings covered part of it, while *persons of interest* filled another section. Passport pictures, or other official ID photos, and surveillance shots of unsuspecting suspects were packed and overlapping every available space.

Whiteboards, covered in hand-written notes about the terrorist group and its members, sat on an adjacent wall. The sloppiness of the writing on the boards, and his being rusty reading French made the information all but useless to Van Pierce.

The RAID task force leader stood at the front of the room and briefed everyone. He spoke mostly French, while the translator relayed the information to the American consultant. Though his reading was rusty, Marvin still had an ear for the language and was able to follow most of it without the help.

"The mission of this new group, known as The Four Serpents is, for all purposes, the same as ISIS, but we believe they are attempting to escalate the levels of conflict," Gavreau said.

"What does that mean?" Ouvrard asked.

"Tracking all known and suspected members, we are finding evidence, through captured emails and phone conversations, that show an interest in increasing the size of their targets and the number of casualties."

"How many members have you found so far?" Van Pierce asked, also speaking French.

"As far as confirmed members, our analysts have discovered these three," Gavreau said, pointing to three photos lined up at the top of the photo wall.

"This is Baasim el-Nazar. He was a known lower-ranking member of ISIS. His move to join the Serpents may have come with a promotion." The photo was a surveillance shot, slightly blurry from being enlarged and zoomed.

"Abdul Ghani al-Basher is an engineer, with a Masters degree in chemistry. We strongly suspect he has built explosive devices used in past terrorist attacks, also for ISIS," Gavreau continued.

The translator continued to speak to Van Pierce as if he didn't understand French, but the American focused on the three photos while listening directly to the RAID Commander.

"Finally, this is Azhaar bin Hashim. He has declared himself the leader of The Four Serpents and has made no attempt to hide his intentions. The problem, however, is that we have almost no information about bin Hashim's past. He has no known connection to any past terrorist activity or group."

Van Pierce narrowed his eyes at this information, and he studied the passport photo.

"Are you sure he's the leader and not just a puppet?" the American asked.

"Unlikely he's a puppet," the computer analyst blurted. "So far, we haven't traced any outgoing signals of any type from bin Hashim that go to anyone other than the lower ranking suspected members."

Van Pierce eyed the young analyst. "Son, there are still effective ways to communicate that are older than cell phones and email."

"Again, unlikely. The amount of coordination to pull off the attacks the Serpents have done in the past, and the ones they are possibly planning in the future, require exact planning and constant communication.

We're confident that Azhaar bin Hashim is the head of the serpent."

Van Pierce stared at the arrogant computer analyst until the man glanced down into the reports on the desk in front of him, then Gavreau continued.

"Our analysts suspect Baasim el-Nazar will meet with someone believed to have financed past terrorist attacks in Europe. We have no identification on this person, except for his alias, Matthias Keppler, which we have learned with the aid of Mr. Van Pierce's US contacts."

Everyone in the room was now studying the notes in front of them, to learn what little they could about the mystery financier.

"There is a high probability that the meeting will take place in the Place des Terreaux, in Lyon, tomorrow. If we can spot el-Nazar and follow him to the meeting, we may be able to identify the financier," Gavreau said.

"It's a very public location. Many tourists," Ouvrard said. "I can't stress the importance of not letting this situation get out of hand."

"Rest assured, sir, we plan to handle the entire operation covertly. Our operatives will be undercover, and will not escalate the conflict unless absolutely necessary," Gavreau said.

Ouvrard still looked a bit nervous but nodded his approval. *I guess that's a universal attitude for all government suits,* Van Pierce thought.

The last few minutes of the meeting were spent giving a general plan the RAID team would take before Gavreau dismissed everyone.

"It all goes down tomorrow, gentlemen. Let's all get some rest," Gavreau said.

* * *

Marvin Van Pierce rubbed his index finger along the bezel of his watch as he checked the time. 09:00 hours. He sat in the passenger seat of a two-door silver Peugeot, parked on the street, one block southwest from Place des Terreaux, between the Saône and Rhône rivers, in Lyon. The crowds grew thicker as more people arrived in the square.

Van Pierce was there that day as an extra set of eyes, and as a consultant to assist if the situation went sideways. It was made very clear to him, by both Maurice Ouvrard and Lionel Gavreau, that he was not to have any physical involvement with today's operation. Being a foreigner, and not an official member of any French police or military organization, they weren't interested in the possibility of an international incident.

In the driver's seat, Simon Boudet, a RAID team member, was radioing updates. Van Pierce didn't have his own radio, so he listened to the responses coming in over Boudet's. Nearly a dozen RAID members positioned themselves in and around the Place des Terreaux. They dressed in civilian clothing and blended in almost entirely. A few blocks away, in a nondescript panel truck, a RAID unit sat in full operational gear, prepared to move in if the situation spun out of control.

Two hours into the operation, radio chatter picked up. A couple of the undercover RAID members spotted Baasim el-Nazar entering the southeast side of the square. Gavreau's voice came in over the channel, advising all teams to keep their eyes open.

Radio communication, from three different undercover operatives following covertly, described the path el-Nazar took through the square. Responses from the other RAID members followed, giving their current position and status.

This continued for the next few minutes, as Marvin glanced up the street toward the Place des Terreaux, even though he wasn't near the radioed positions. He scanned everyone, looking for postures or behaviors that might appear suspicious. It was a habit he gained from many years in the field and was now second nature for him.

It was because of this awareness that a face in the crowd triggered an alarm in his head. A man, with a jagged scar that across his cheek, walked right passed the silver Peugeot, and into a crowd of tourists.

Van Pierce snatched up his smartphone and scrolled through the photos from yesterday's briefing. His fingers froze on an image of a man with the same scar and intense eyes. It was Zain al-Aman, someone the French government suspected of being a member of The Four Serpents, but they couldn't verify. His appearance in this place at this time was just too much to be a coincidence.

"That man there," Van Pierce said to his partner in the car. "That's Zain al-Aman. We need someone on him now."

Boudet nodded and radioed in the request. Van Pierce tried to keep a visual on his target, as the radio responses came.

"This is Unit Two. I can be there in three minutes."

"That's not fast enough. He's gonna disappear in that crowd," Van Pierce said, knowing how far they were positioned from the square.

Without hesitation, he opened the door to follow al-Aman.

"Sir, you can't—" Boudet began before he was cut off.

"Let the team know I'm tailing al-Aman. Have them coordinate with me when they reach my location," Van Pierce said, then he slipped into the crowd of people.

* * *

Gavreau was positioned outside the Place des Terreaux, in a discreet position that gave him a broad view of the area. He gritted his teeth at the call he just received from Boudet. Marvin Van Pierce was actively pursuing a man that may be on their list of suspected terrorist group members.

Gavreau didn't want anyone but RAID personnel active in the area.

Van Pierce was experienced, but the possible confusion and chaos of having a foreigner, a civilian at that, active in the operation didn't sit well with the task force leader. Still, without the American's help, Gavreau's team may not have spotted the extra player.

Van Pierce didn't have a radio with him, however, which made the situation even more frustrating. After a moment of thought, he thumbed his own radio.

"Unit Two, as soon as you get there, you relieve Mr. Van Pierce and have him stand down."

"Oui." The response came over the radio quickly.

Gavreau set his focus back on observing the square while listening to the updates from the team following el-Nazar.

"—heading toward the cafe, on the east side of the fountain. This might be the meeting spot," one of the RAID members said.

"Alright, stay on him and let us know if he leaves. All units, I want you to scan everyone in the area. Find anyone that might be there to meet him," Gavreau said.

After a minute of updates being radioed in, one transmission caught the task leader's attention.

"El-Nazar made contact with someone. They split up, the new target is moving southeast."

Gavreau prepared to coordinate his team to account for the new player when the radio channels lit up.

"He's got a bomb!"

"El-Nazar—"

The radio transmission cut off a split second before Gavreau heard the explosions.

* * *

Marvin Van Pierce worked his way through the crowd, tailing his target from a reasonable distance. He was a little rusty from years of not being out in the field, but found his skills were recalled pretty easily.

Al-Aman crossed the street and entered the Place des Terreaux from the southwest corner. He stayed on the outer edge, slowing and eventually stopping. He glanced around casually across the public square.

A tremendous sculptured fountain, the Fontaine Bartholdi, dominated the center of the Place des Terreaux. It featured a woman on a chariot, controlling four horses, each representing the four great rivers of France. Crowds gathered around the sculpture, sitting at the outdoor tables set up under canopies for the nearby restaurants.

Al-Aman turned his gaze toward Marvin, but Van Pierce was sure to not make eye contact with his target, instead, pretending to study the large fountain in the square.

Next, Van Pierce swept his gaze across the area, looking for the other RAID members. There were too many people around for him to make a positive ID on any of them, however.

When he looked back, he saw al-Aman reaching into the inner pocket of his jacket. Van Pierce moved closer, his focus like a laser on his target. Panicked voices suddenly screamed out from across the square.

In the next instant, they were cut off by a deafening explosion.

Van Pierce tore his eyes off al-Aman, and toward the blast. He felt the concussive force press against his chest, even this far away from the explosion, and saw smoke and dust rising in the northeast corner of the square, just past the fountain. Confusion and fear took the crowd. Then it turned to outright chaos and panic when the second blast went off.

He saw the second explosion this time. It was a suicide bomber, also on the far side of the square, in the southeast corner. While he turned his attention back to al-Aman, Van Pierce whipped his hand to the back of his right hip, a pure reflex, and found the spot where he carried his pistol for so many years empty. He saw his target holding a small device now, staring into the crowd of people.

The two explosions caused a panic as terror washed over everyone like the fire and heat from the blasts themselves. They ran away from the death and destruction, and out of the square. Sudden horror dawned on Van Pierce. The two explosions had occurred on the other end of the public square, detonated in a position that would force the panicked bystanders to move in this direction. Lambs led to the slaughter. Right into the position of al-Aman, the third bomber.

Van Pierce cursed himself for being too late to catch the attacks, but he sprang into action, knowing he had to do something right now. He bolted for al-Aman, shoving people away, and shouting a warning to the bystanders. He shot in low and buried his shoulder into al-Aman's midsection. The momentum of his body carried the man off his feet.

Van Pierce wouldn't be able to stop this blast, but he would try to minimize the damage it could cause. He plowed the man into the street, between a panel truck and a van that stopped after the first explosion.

The two men landed partially under the delivery truck when the explosives engulfed al-Aman and Van Pierce in fire and fury.

Head of the Serpent

The Manning Brothers

CHAPTER

3

"At approximately eleven a.m. local time, nine a.m. Greenwich Mean Time, three men detonated explosives devices strapped to their bodies, in the Place des Terreaux, located in Lyon, France.

John stared at his television in silence, watching the news report about the terrorist attack in France.

"The damage in the public square is extensive. Ten people have been confirmed dead at this time, and at least fifty people have been injured by the blasts. Once again, The Four Serpents have claimed responsibility for this horrific terrorist attack. In a video statement released—"

A sense of dread formed in the pit of his stomach. John stood and walked to the phone, each step only serving to intensify his fears. He had to call to make sure Marvin Van Pierce was okay. The phone rang right as he grabbed hold of it.

John closed his eyes and brought the receiver up to his ear. "Hello."

"John, it's Parker,"

Hearing Parker Lewis' voice confirmed his worst fears. Before joining the Hostile Response Division, John had saved Parker's life. He was a brilliant if eccentric computer specialist for the HRD.

"Parker. I need to call Van Pierce. He may be hurt," John said.

"John, I—I'm sorry. Van Pierce is dead," Parker said.

John's fist tightened over the phone receiver, nearly crushing it in his grip. Deep down he knew it was the truth. Parker wouldn't be calling John to get more information. If he was calling, that meant he already knew the situation.

"Are you sure?" John asked, holding out hope that his gut was wrong.

"Yes. Marvin told me about his assignment after he spoke with you. The moment I heard the news about the attack, I scoured around for everything I could about it. Officers on the scene confirmed his identity 10 minutes ago. It hasn't gone public yet."

Numbness set in, as John's vision swam. He clutched the phone tighter and sat at the chair next to the small table.

"Are you alright, John?" Parker asked.

John sat in silence for what felt like hours, before finally answering.

"I should have gone with him. If I was there, maybe—"

"There's nothing you could have done. It was a coordinated attack that no one was prepared for. If you were there with Marvin, you might be dead too."

John knew Parker was right but had a hard time accepting it. Parker's words hit John deeply, but at that moment he had made a decision.

"I'm going to France. I need to know what happened," John said, resigned.

"John, what do you think you can accomplish there? We aren't with the HRD anymore. Just stay there, and I'll find out what I can," Parker said. *"Please."*

John's neck and jaw tightened. "I'm leaving tonight."

"Then let me come with you. I can help," Parker started.

"No, it's dangerous. I don't want you to risk your life over this," John said.

"But it's okay if you do?" Parker asked.

"This isn't your responsibility. I could have helped Van Pierce, but now I need answers. I owe him that much."

Parker let out a sigh on the other end. *"Alright John, please be careful. Let me know if there's anything I can do to help. I owe him too."*

CHAPTER

4

Shoulders brushing the walls of the narrow alleyway, a burly man strode through the back entrance of a small printing shop. The whirring and clattering of machines replaced the bustle of activity from outside. The man widened his eyes, waiting for them to adjust to the darkness before proceeding.

He stepped into a backroom, shuffled to one corner, and greeted three men sitting around a table. The man facing him, Azhaar bin Hashim, nodded as he took another drag from his cigarette.

"Praise be to Allah," the man said with his head bowed.

"What do you have for me?" bin Hashim asked as smoke puffed out between syllables.

The man produced a small tablet computer. He tapped the screen a few times and handed the device over to the leader.

Bin Hashim examined the information, the blue LED glow lighting his face from underneath, casting his features with a more sinister appearance. Satisfied, he nodded and placed the device casually on the center of the table.

"Is this information accurate?" he asked.

"Yes. We have confirmation that the German survived," the man said.

Bin Hashim thought over the information for a minute, taking another drag from his cigarette.

He blew out a stream of smoke. "Send someone to *Hôpital de la Croix-Rousse*. Find the German, and finish what we started," bin Hashim said. "The next phase of our plan is too important. We must tie up all loose ends."

The man nodded to the leader of the Four Serpents, and walked out, exiting through the back door where he entered.

"What should we do now?" one of the other men at the table asked.

"Proceed as planned. The doctor will be in town soon. Have the men ready to move when they hear from me," bin Hashim said, stabbing the butt of the cigarette into the ashtray.

The men nodded and stood. Bin Hashim could see they all knew what was expected of them, working toward the same goal. He clutched the medallion around his neck, four snakes entwined around the world, before tucking it into his shirt.

The Four Serpents would strike fear into the hearts of the west. They would crush the spirit of the enemy. The world would not be able to deny them for long.

CHAPTER

5

Lyon, France

Grabbing his bag and looping the strap over his shoulder, John draped his light jacket over one arm as he stepped out of the cab. He had difficulty sleeping on the long flight, thinking about Van Pierce and the terrorist attack from the previous day.

His head hurt, and his joints creaked and protested as he stretched on the sidewalk. Knowing the police would have the area restricted, John had to walk the several remaining blocks to the Place des Terreaux. While the city was far from busy, the amount of activity near the attack surprised John.

He got a feel for the block and the people as he approached his destination. The pain and fear evident in their actions, the people carried out their day to day activities nonetheless. An act of defiance showing the terrorists that they were still strong and unafraid after the attack.

John brought only a laptop, and a change of clothes, on top of the few travel necessities with him, opting to travel light. Everything he needed was with him in the bag around his shoulder. Except for a weapon. He knew traveling abroad meant going in unarmed, but he didn't expect a second attack in the same location so soon.

Much of the initial investigation had already happened the day before, but the police still had the entire block taped off. Investigators buzzed around, gathering evidence at the blast sites, and taking pictures of everything that appeared out of place.

Several officers diverted traffic to different routes, creating more confusion and congestion. The honking and understandable frustration gave John enough cover to get closer. He walked the perimeter of the Place des Terreaux, looking over the area and paying particular attention to the three locations where the terrorists detonated their bombs.

During the flight, he pored over all of the information Parker sent him, including news stories providing an already out of date account of the events of the attack. He crossed the police barrier to look at the spot where the third device went off, studying the two vehicles damaged in the explosion.

The blast pattern revealed that the device exploded under the back end of the more massive truck. The detonation shredded the tires and left the rear bumper in shambles. The entire back end of the vehicle crumpled upward. Bits of broken glass littered the street and sidewalk, from the shattered windows of both trucks and the nearby shops.

This is where Marvin Van Pierce died. John took a moment to reflect on the man. They had known each other only for a short time, but Van Pierce still risked his life and career to save him, and clear his name, when John faced treason charges. Tightening his fists, John vowed that he would find the ones responsible for Marvin Van Pierce's death.

According to Parker's reports, Van Pierce's final act of sacrifice had saved many more lives. Tackling the suicide bomber under the truck contained a significant portion of the blast, significantly reducing the number of casualties the third blast caused to the frightened people fleeing the first two explosions.

"A hero to the end," John said quietly, looking to the clear blue sky.

"Que fais-tu ici?" a voice snapped John out of his thoughts.

He turned to see a stern man in black fatigues and gloves. He wore a tactical vest, with a name tag that read *Gavreau*. John hadn't spoken French in many years, and he was caught off guard for a moment.

"I'm sorry, I don't speak—"

33

"What are you doing here?" Gavreau interrupted, speaking heavily accented English now. "This is no place for tourists right now."

"Just looking around. My friend was here yesterday," John said.

Gavereau furrowed his brow. "This is still an active crime scene. You cannot be here right now."

"His name was Marvin Van Pierce. He was here working as a consultant with you," John said.

The man's face softened, and his tone changed to match.

"I am sorry, sir, but you cannot be here. This area is not open to the public right now. You must go," Gavreau said.

The two stood to face each other for a few tense seconds. Gavreau was every inch as tall as John, though his build was leaner than the Ranger's muscular bulk. Another man in the same military-style uniform walked at a brisk pace toward Gavreau. His name tag read *Brassard*.

They spoke in French using lowered voices so John couldn't hear, much less understand, what was being said.

"Let me help," John said. "I worked with Van Pierce, and I have experience dealing with terrorists."

Gavreau looked up from his conversation. "No, we do not need your help. This is official police business."

"Alright. If it's okay with you, I'd like to look around just a little more. I won't step on any toes."

"We cannot have civilians in our crime scene," Gavereau said. "We do not want to deal with the international problems if an *American tourist* got hurt nosing around. Stay out of this, or I will have you arrested."

Brassard spoke to John. "I apologize, sir, but this situation is delicate. We must ask you to move beyond the barrier around this square, please." His English had almost no accent, and his tone was calmer.

John nodded to Brassard and Gavreau, then turned and left the Place des Terreaux.

He had no intention of *staying out of this*, but for now, he would have to operate from the shadows to avoid arrest. He shouldered his bag and pulled out his phone to arrange for a cab to take him to a hotel.

From there, he would be able to dig deeper into Parker's research, using what he saw on site to put more of the pieces together, and gain a better understanding of the events that transpired.

CHAPTER

6

John sat at the small desk in his hotel room. He opted for the most basic of comforts, a single bed, bathroom, and mini office. By all accounts, this room would be considered more cozy than utilitarian, but it served all his needs for now.

The laptop beeped and whirred as it came to life, ready to work. John wanted to reread the data Parker sent before he left, but enough time had passed that footage from other people in the area started popping up online.

He watched every available video, sometimes bringing two different videos side by side, in order to build a mental picture of the attack. Parker wasn't able to secure any of the footage from the CCTV cameras mounted around the scene, so he had to watch only way was publicly available, uploaded to various social media and video sharing sites.

All of the footage had been taken by mobile phones or handheld cameras. In the chaos and confusion, it was difficult for John to make heads or tails of the necessary details he needed. Without any type of image stabilization, discerning directions, or even number of attackers was next to impossible.

Rubbing his temples and then his eyes with his fingertips, John felt every second of the two hours he had just spent watching and re-watching the videos that he thought held the most promise. Still, it was a futile venture. "This is going to be impossible without the footage from the city's cameras."

The old wooden chair creaked as John leaned back, folding his arms across his chest. He took in a deep breath to calm his mind. *Perhaps a few hours of sleep would do me some good,* he thought. *Maybe by then Parker will be able to—*

A new notification popped up in his search. The latest video from the terrorist attack sat at the top of his queue, and the quality of the thumbnail image gave him a small boost of energy.

John watched the video, taken near the first explosion, in the northwest corner of the Place des Terreaux. The clarity of the footage gave him hope, but so far it was all just information he had been able to piece together in his initial research. A crowd of people dined near the Fontaine Bertholdi when a man stood up and detonated an explosive device on his person.

John sighed, ready to close the video, when he stopped himself, finger hovering over the touchpad. Something caught his attention, at a subconscious level, but he didn't know why.

He viewed the footage again, scrubbing the timeline back and forth, studying the screen for any details he may have missed. It was the moment before the blast when he noticed the man seated at a table next to the bomber.

The terrorist and the mystery man sat back to back at different tables, but the mystery man was already moving away from him before the detonation. The timing of his movement felt out of place to John. His actions didn't fit the sequence of events.

The man rose from his table and moved away much earlier than anyone else in the crowd. Before the bomber even physically revealed any evidence of his explosive. Something spooked him. When the terrorist stood, he turned and directed his attention to the mystery man.

Who are you?" John said, staring at the paused frame.

The footage was too blurry to make a positive identification, so John checked through all of the videos he felt provided the best information during his initial viewing. He singled out all of the footage that pointed in the direction of the Fontaine Bertholdi before, during, and after the attack.

On the third video, he hit pay dirt. A tourist standing on the opposite side filmed the statue as the first explosive detonated. John saw the mystery man running from the bomber, toward the camera.

The footage shook and dropped from the explosion, then panned back to the site of the blast. The mystery man emerged from inside the fountain, soaking wet. He somehow managed to leap into the water to escape the brunt of the explosion.

The tourist continued filming as he backed away. The crowd ran past him, parting long enough for John to get a better angle on the man's features. John rewound the video and paused it.

His jaw tightened. The mystery man was long suspected of financing terrorist activities. Even during John's years serving as an Army Ranger, they sought this man in the war on terror. He was known under different aliases, but the one John was most familiar with was Dietrich Werner.

If this is the man John suspected he was, why were they trying to kill him in the terrorist attack? Did he manage to survive the second and third blasts as well? It was possible, which meant Werner could still be out there.

John pulled up a list of all of the videos showing the second and third explosions, carefully attempting to track Werner's movements during and after the attack. He found a far camera shot of the third explosion, shot from outside the Place des Terreaux, on a connecting street.

He spotted the man moving away from the first two explosions, in the general direction of the third. John's heart sank when he saw the blurred movements of a figure that moved to tackle another man. Marvin Van Pierce putting himself in harm's way to try and stop the third bomber.

Marvin sacrificed himself to save as many as he could. He had been able to take the man down, near two parked vehicles, which absorbed much of the explosive force when the bomb detonated.

At the moment of the blast, John caught an image of Dietrich falling. It was only a couple of frames, but he was close to the final explosion. Van Pierce's actions may have reduced the force enough for the man to survive. If he were still alive, he would need medical attention, given his proximity to the first and third bombs.

John dug through the files Parker sent him to read on the flight over. He needed more information about Dietrich Werner. Why would the Four Serpents be targeting him? Was his presence a coincidence.

A single reference came up, a list of known aliases for a person of interest. Dietrich was one of many aliases used by Matthias Keppler, the man Marvin Van Pierce highlighted in the briefing notes that Parker had been able to retrieve.

"Mister Keppler," John said, resting his elbows on the desk as he stared at the image in the video. "Perhaps we'll finally be able to meet face to face, so you can answer some questions."

The latest news reports about the attack mentioned that first responders had transported the injured people to Hôpital de la Croix-Rousse. He closed the screen of his laptop and headed out the door to find his next lead.

* * *

The hallways of Hôpital de la Croix-Rousse swarmed with activity. Doctors and nurses sped around the concerned friends and family members of the injured tourists and citizens. Kaliq, a member of the Four Serpents, had no trouble slipping into the supply area to get a set of scrubs to wear in the ensuing confusion.

He came here with explicit orders to find Matthias Keppler. Dressing as hospital staff was risky, but dealing with the seemingly non-stop flow of victims

41

helped him slip through unquestioned. Several times someone barked orders at him to go somewhere and assist, or bring something that one of the doctors needed. Each time he answered with an enthusiastic nod before disappearing.

Matthias Keppler secretly funded Azhaar bin Hashim and the Four Serpents, through his many shell companies, for their next ambitious plan. Bin Hashim didn't trust a man of Keppler's questionable loyalties and planned for his death in the attack on Place des Terreaux.

Kaliq stepped behind an unattended reception desk and sat in front of the computer. His fingers danced across keys, searching for Keppler's room, as the switches of the old keyboard clicked loudly. His brows furrowed when the name came up with no results.

His target, it seems, was also the type of man to cover his tracks. Matthias Keppler was probably the type of man with a list of aliases to use in his day to day life. Paranoid.

After a moment of thought, Kaliq's hands flew over the keys again. He brought up a list of the patients admitted into the hospital shortly after yesterday's attack. He scanned through the results, memorizing the rooms where the most recent patients had been admitted.

Kaliq stood and stepped back into the hallway, passing someone as he exited. The woman gave him a quizzical look as she sat, but soon slipped back into the task at hand, dealing with another influx of patients.

He glanced down at the chart for the man and woman admitted to the first room. The victims in the beds had been badly burnt. Their bodies bandaged and they were heavily medicated. Not finding his mark, he turned and left, side-stepping a nurse coming in to check on their vital stats.

Finding his target would require that he search the rooms one by one. This would not be a problem for him. He was a patient man that operated with precision.

It would not be long before he cleaned up the loose end, Keppler, before he could reveal anything he might know about the Serpents or their next plan.

CHAPTER
7

John walked into the hospital and looked across the lobby. He wasn't sure how he would find Dietrich Werner in here, but this was his best shot.

John stopped the nearest staff member. "Excuse me," John said to the young woman dressed in scrubs. "I'm wondering if you can help me find someone."

The woman stared back with weary eyes, replying in French.

John winced, not able to understand anything she said. He continued in English, speaking slower and hoping the woman would understand enough to help him out.

"My brother was hurt yesterday," John started, miming an explosion with his hands.

The woman seemed to catch on to what he was saying, so he continued. "He is supposed to be here. Where can I find him?"

They struggled to communicate, as her English was as bad as his French. But eventually, she directed him to the wing of the hospital triaging everyone involved in yesterday's terrorist attack. John thanked the woman in English and then again in passable French. She smiled and excused herself to continue her work.

John sighed as he looked down the crowded hall. This would be a little more complicated than expected. John didn't let the difficulty dissuade him. As an Army Ranger, he was always prepared for things to be more challenging than initially planned.

He walked down the hallway, heading for the section of the hospital the woman described. His initial urge was to ask any and everybody where he would go to find his *brother* injured in the attack, but John wanted to stay under the radar. The last thing he wanted was to draw any unnecessary attention to him right now.

He made his way through the hospital until the people in and around him looked like they were all there for the same reason, suffering from similar burns, cuts, and bruises typical of injuries inflicted by an explosion.

Distraught friends and family packed the waiting areas, in need of treatment, or hoping for any good news from the doctors and nurses. People agitated at the lack of information or attention they were receiving. Anger, fear, frustration.

John made his way to a receptionist desk and tried again to find his *brother*. He made an attempt at foregoing English and speaking French, ultimately having to resort to a mix of the two languages to get his message across.

Luck was on his side this time, as the man replied in English. "I am sorry to hear about your brother. What is his name?"

"Werner. Dietrich Werner," John said.

The man typed a few keystrokes then stared at the screen for a minute. He leaned in close before sitting back and typing something else. His brows furrowed.

"I don't see a Werner, but there is a Dietrich Byrne, similar name, but—"

"That's him," John interrupted with a relieved smile. "I forgot he's using Byrne for his businesses. I'm sorry, my mind is a little frazzled after..." He waved his hand briefly in the air, resisting the urge to over-explain the situation, knowing it would only cause more suspicion and confusion.

"I, uh, okay. Dietrich is in room 513. It is on the fifth floor—"

"Thank you, I can find it," John interrupted again as he turned to go.

Before the man could suspect any foul play, an irate husband demanded to speak to a doctor to find out what was happening with his wife, giving John the cover he needed to slip away.

* * *

Kaliq spent the past hour in the hospital, moving room to room. He glanced into each doorway, trying to find the man he was sent to kill. The German financier was too involved in the Serpents' actions. He knew too much, and bin Hashim's plans were too important to allow anyone to put them at risk.

Anyone else in Kaliq's shoes would succumb to the frustration and fatigue, with such a repetitive task. He was a special breed, however. The thrill of this hunt fueled him. His whole life, he was always precise and technical in everything he did. He rarely suffered the type of mental fatigue that others would experience after long hours of repetitious tasks.

He continued the door to door hunt, searching for his target, and continually moving with the same mannerisms of the hospital staff around him. That was another skill he learned when he was a young boy. Kaliq always had a knack for picking out and remembering subtle physical details and mannerisms of people, allowing him to mimic his friends and family.

Now on the fifth floor of the hospital, Kaliq resumed his mission. On the fourth door he checked, he saw a man in one of the beds with a build similar to Keppler. The chart listed the man as Dietrich Byrne. The Serpent slipped into the room, making sure no one else was in there to disturb the two of them.

Once he approached, Kaliq saw that this was indeed Matthias Keppler, admitted under an alias. He walked to the side of the bed and stared into the face of the man as he slept.

Dietrich groaned and opened his eyes slowly, turning his head to look over at Kaliq. Keppler mistook him as a nurse at first glance as he struggled to keep his eyes open. The assassin continued to stare down at the person in the bed, patiently waiting for recognition to set in. He wanted Dietrich, Keppler, to know his end was coming.

Realization struck as the man's eyes flew open wide. Because of the internal damage he suffered in the final explosion, the doctors had hooked Keppler up to a respirator. Unable to scream for help, he clawed at the side of his bed, searching for the button to call the nurses for assistance.

Kaliq looked on in amusement for another few seconds with a sadistic grin and held the button up by its cord in his hand. He shook his head and made a *tsk tsk* sound. He placed the switch on a side table, to of reach, and descended on Matthias Keppler.

* * *

Lionel Gavreau strode down the corridor of the fifth floor of the Hôpital de la Croix-Rousse. He stopped and leaned against a wall, swiping up through the endless barrage of messages and emails. The bureaucrats overseeing RAID and its investigation into the terrorist attack bombarded him with non-stop requests and demands for more information.

None of that mattered to him at this moment. He was here for his teammates now. Several members of his RAID team suffered injuries in the blasts at the Place des Terreaux yesterday. Two were currently in critical condition. Gavreau had been in the hospital for the past hour, waiting for any updates on his injured teammates.

He dropped the phone into a jacket pocket and rocked his head side to side, cracking his neck with each movement. It did little to hold the fatigue at bay.

Gavreau stepped into in the room of a man with minor injuries from the attack. His man had a concussion, and the doctors wanted him kept under observation. He had his bed upright and was surfing through the television stations, looking for something to watch other than coverage of the terrorist attack.

"You don't have to stay here, sir," Alban Lussier said to his commander.

"Don't worry, I'm not concerned about you. I'm just in here so no one bothers me, while I wait to hear about the teammates I actually like," Gavreau said.

Lussier laughed and thumbed the TV remote, finally settling on a rerun of Friends, dubbed in French.

"I'm going to get a coffee, want anything?" Gavreau asked on his way out.

"A cigarette," the man answered. The RAID Commander shook his head and stepped into the hallway.

With the chaos of yesterday's attack settling down, the crowds had thinned, but the hospital was still buzzing with plenty of activity. Gavreau headed down the hall, toward a vending machine, when a man leaving one of the rooms caught his eye.

He was a large, muscular man in jeans and a thin long sleeve shirt. There was no mistaking the heavy mustache visible from the man's profile. It was the American wandering the crime scene this morning.

The activity around the room the American had just left suddenly picked up. That was when Gavreau noticed the constant beep of flatlining patient whistling through the door. Nurses flooded into the room, followed by a doctor, treating the patient in his bed.

Everyone nearby showed an expected level of curiosity and concern in a situation like this. Except for the American. The big man moved away, quickly down the hall, as close to a near run as he could manage without alerting anyone around him.

Gavreau had no such concerns as he charged down the hallway after the suspicious man. It was no coincidence that he would be crossing paths with the man twice, both times related to the terrorist attack. He pushed people out of his way as he moved down the corridor.

The American was not difficult to track, as he was much larger than most of the people around him. But even with fewer people wandering around, Gavreau had difficulty moving through the crowd efficiently.

The RAID leader increased his pace and began shouting at the people near him to get clear, when he saw his target slip around a corner, out of sight. Gavreau was losing patience, and shoved people forcefully out of his way, as he struggled to catch the man. The aggressive actions only served to agitate the

51

already stressed people in the hospital around Gavreau.

Just great, Gavreau thought. The additional anger and confusion were only going to make his job that much harder.

* * *

John exited the elevator on the fifth floor and turned toward *Dietrich Byrne's* room. He looked around and saw RAID members in the hallways. John kept his head down and walked briskly past them. They were most likely here to see to the members of their team injured, so he didn't want to aggravate them anymore.

The room he was looking for was not far, but there was a lot of police around so it would be difficult to get in and out of unless he was utterly discreet about it. He found door 513 and scouted it patiently. After several minutes no medical staff had entered or exited. John moved toward the room.

He didn't expect to see any doctors or nurses inside, so it caught John off guard when he saw the man in medical scrubs stepping out, just as he was about to step in. He paused for a moment, looking away to avoid attracting the attention of the man.

When he was in the clear once more, John stepped into the room.

Stepping just inside, he stopped, processing what he saw. Matthias lay still in his bed, eyes open. At first, John thought the man was focused on the TV, and not paying attention to him entering the room. Only, the TV wasn't on. In the hall, over the crowds talking and the noise from the increased activity in the hospital at that moment, John didn't hear the heart rate monitor. Once he stepped into the room, the sustained beep was loud and clear, a siren going off to alert everyone in the hospital.

John cursed. He needed to leave, now. The noise in the hall quieted down, once the people nearby finally heard the beeping. Someone called for a doctor. John turned to leave but hesitated. He saw the clothes of the dead man, in a chair next to the bed. Hoping for something that could keep his investigation going, he snatched the man's wallet. Perhaps it might lead John to the next clue.

Half expecting the man in the scrubs to come back into the room, John started in the opposite direction as he exited. When he stepped out, nurses and doctors filed past to get into the room. He caught a glimpse of the man in scrubs leaving the scene. John paused for a beat, watching him. He was the only medical staff near the room to not turn back and help.

Suspicion overtook John, and he followed the man. He moved quickly, without going into a full run, to avoid suspicion. He tried to gain on the man in the scrubs, catching only brief glimpses of his curly hair cut close along the sides. The man was smaller, able to slip past the crowds in the hall with little difficulty. His uncanny ability to read the movement of the people around him and avoid a collision was a stark contrast to John's broad frame nearly knocking the people in the crowd down as he walked through.

John continued to push past as delicately as he could, but he was losing the man in the scrubs. Once he rounded the next corner, John increased his speed. He knocked down one of the patients accidentally, who let out an angry cry, and almost stopped to help the person. Unfortunately, the sound of the patient yelling caught the attention of the target John was pursuing.

The man in the scrubs turned and looked John right in the eye. He looked impassive, unsurprised even when he found out he was being followed. The man simply turned and started to run through the hallway, now finding the crowds thinning out. John began to pick up his own pace when he heard someone else yelling behind him.

"Stop!" the voice said.

John didn't slow down, instead turning his head to see who was shouting. The RAID agent from earlier today, Gavreau, was moving toward John. He must have seen John leave room 513 and suspected him of killing Matthias. John had to keep going, or he would lose the real person responsible for Dietrich Werner's death.

He shouldered his way into the empty parts of the hall and broke into a full run. The man in the scrubs turned down another hall, trying to lose his tail. John followed around the corner and didn't see the man. He glanced around, scanning for anything that stood out. A door just clicked shut a moment after he turned the corner.

John stepped through that same door, stepping into a series of connected examination rooms with a small corridor running between them, with an exit door located at the far end of the hall.

John resisted the urge to plow ahead to the door on the far end, and possibly allowing the man to slip behind him to double back. He did a quick visual search of each room on his way to the far exit. Halfway down the corridor, John pushed the curtain open to inspect the next room.

A figure burst out, catching him off guard. A kick thrust into the center of John's chest with enough force to steal his breath and knock him back several steps.

The man landed and continued a rapid-fire assault on the much larger American. Compared to John, he lacked the size and strength for a straight up fight, but his speed and technique made him formidable. John used his muscular forearms to deflect and absorb the incoming attacks, and he cursed to himself, as he could only stop two out of every three strikes.

John fired back his own punches, his heavy fists finding only air. A front kick shot through John's defenses, driving into his stomach. The speed and power of the attack pushed him back on his heels into a cart filled with supplies.

The man in scrubs took the opportunity to make a break for the far corridor exit. John reached behind him and hurled the entire supply cart at the fleeing man. It crashed into his back, sending him sprawling with a yelp. John lunged forward and brought a stomp down on his target. The man barely rolled away as a heavy boot cracked the tile flooring.

In one smooth turn, the man on the floor whipped a roundhouse kick across John's jaw and spun to his feet. John reached for him, dazed, but he rolled up and over, across John's back. The man hit the floor and dashed toward the original door they entered through. John shook the cobwebs from his head and spun to pursue.

John crashed out through the door, heading back into the hospital to find his target, but caught the attention of Gavreau. The RAID commander followed the sound of the commotion and arrived to see the American emerge into the hallway.

"Stop right now!" Gavreau yelled in heavily accented English.

John was in an awkward spot now. He needed to find the man responsible for killing Keppler, but running away from Gavreau would do nothing to prove his own innocence. Not having time to explain, John turned and bolted down the hall, away from Gavreau.

The RAID man cursed and gave chase. Despite John's size, he was a surprisingly fast runner, and his conditioning was more than up to the task of carrying his heavy frame at a run. Gavreau was leaner, and quicker however, closing the distance.

John had to guess where the man in scrubs could have gone while keeping away from Gavreau. He sprinted toward the nearest stairwell, figuring the man was attempting to leave the building. Gavreau was closing fast, and before John could get through the stairwell door, the RAID commander was on top of him.

Gavreau collided with John, and they both spilled into the stairwell. The momentum of the two large men carried them down the steps, to the landing halfway down one flight. Gavreau rolled, trying to gain the top position. John shot a muscular arm out and pulled the Frenchman to the ground, while he got up to one knee.

"I'm sorry about this," John said before his fist cracked across Gavreau's jaw.

The commander went limp, and John tried to lay him down as gently as he could, before resuming his chase. He continued down the stairs, and into the first-floor lobby.

John looked around everywhere, trying to find any clues about where to find the man. Nothing. He went outside and scanned in every direction. His quarry had vanished. He ground his jaw tight, furious at losing both his target and the fight against him.

John had to flee the area. He would most likely be a murder suspect, and fighting with Gavreau would definitely not help the situation.

Once he was far enough from the hospital, John stepped into an alley and rifled through the wallet, finding an ID for Dietrich Byrne. He had no guarantee that the address listed wasn't fake, but John didn't have any other options at this point.

He considered going back to his hotel room to check out, in case the police were looking for him. There was little doubt the **RAID** man he knocked out would discover his identity and begin searching for him.

If he didn't follow his one lead, however, he might lose his only chance to stop the Four Serpents before they strike again.

CHAPTER

8

Gavreau rubbed his jaw with one hand. Clenching his teeth harder only served to intensify the pain, but his anger won out as he breathed deeply, in and out through flared nostrils. The American had gotten away, but not before assaulting the RAID commander. *For that, you will pay dearly.*

In the security room of the hospital, Gavreau reviewed the video footage covering the fifth floor, specifically the camera that provided a few of 513. The room where the victim, Dietrich Byrne, had been murdered. He watched the American exit into the hall, as nurses and doctors flooded in, past him.

"Run the feed back a few minutes," Gavreau said through still clenched teeth.

The security tech nodded and complied.

"There. Stop." Gavreau pointed at the screen.

They watched for a minute until he saw what caught his attention while the tech rewound the footage. A man wearing hospital scrubs entered the room.

"Who is that?" Gavreau asked.

A hospital administrator leaned closer to examine the feed. "I don't know this man. I'll get the records of everyone on the floor and find out."

You may not find him, Gavreau thought.

The man looked like a staff member of the hospital, but something about him triggered an alarm in Gavreau's head.

No one else entered or exited the room for a couple of minutes until the American entered the frame for the first time. Gavreau's jaw ached and tightened when he saw him.

He watched the man walk past the RAID members in the hall, his head low, heading straight for room 513. The man in scrubs exited, walking right past the American.

Gavreau focused on the man in the hospital scrubs this time. He noted the man continued to walk away, not reacting to the frantic nurses running by him, or the flatlining beep Gavreau remembered hearing at that moment.

"Perhaps it was you," he said, his voice low.

The American, after exiting the room, spotted the man in the scrubs and moved straight in his direction.

Shortly after, the footage showed Gavreau running to catch up to them.

Christopher Brassard entered the security room with a few sheets of paper in his hand.

"Sir, here is the information you requested," he said, handing them over.

Gavreau took the papers and looked over the information about the identity of the American.

"John Stone. A Lieutenant, serving in the United States Army for twenty years. Most of that time, he served as an Army Ranger. Recipient of the Distinguished Service Cross," Brassard said as Gavreau read the report.

He continued to scan the pages. After he retired from the Army, Stone worked at a bar in Great Falls, Montana, of which he was also a part owner. Gavreau saw the news stories Brassard printed, about the kidnapping of a girl, Emily Colt. He read about John Stone's involvement, rescuing her from her kidnappers.

Shortly after that, Stone officially joined a joint military task force called the Hostile Response Division. Gavreau skimmed the brief history of the HRD, and its Director, Marvin Van Pierce.

"Sir, I don't think he was the one responsible for killing Dietrich Byrne, the man in 513," Brassard said.

Gavreau grunted. He figured that was the case, and the video footage, with this report, confirmed it for him.

"Don't expect me to cheer for this John Stone, Chris," Gavreau said, absently touching his jaw again.

"What next?" Brassard asked.

"Find out more about Dietrich in room 513. Why was he targeted?" Gavreau said.

Brassard held out another sheet of paper. "Right here, sir."

Gavreau took the page with a surprised look on his face and nodded.

"Dietrich Byrne, a German businessman. Currently living in—" Brassard started.

Gavreau shot a glare at his second-in-command. "Why do you hand me these papers if you're just going to read them to me?" Gavreau asked.

"Sorry," Brassard said with a smile. "My job is to provide you with information."

"Well, our next move is to find out everything we can about Dietrich Byrne. Chris, get the authorization we need to search his residence, and meet me outside."

"Yes, sir."

Gavreau headed toward the elevator, rereading the report about John Stone, working his jaw side to side to make sure it wasn't fractured. *That man hits harder than a truck.*

* * *

Somewhere near Lyon, France

At Matthias Keppler's address, John walked the block an once more. He scouted for any sign of police, or terrorists, satisfied that the streets were clear.

He carried a brown paper bag with groceries from a nearby market, to help him appear as if he belonged in the neighborhood. The delicious aroma from the still warm baguette protruding from the bag reminded John that he hadn't eaten anything for quite a while now.

Leafy greens swayed gently with each step as John walked casually to the front entrance of the apartment building. He pretended to check his phone, waiting for a moment to time his entry.

A woman exited, and John started walking, still pretending to stare at the screen on his phone as he approached. The woman offered to hold the door open to let him in.

He smiled and nodded as he passed the woman, not wanting to risk saying anything in French. He made his way to the stairs and started up to Keppler's floor. Taking the steps two at a time, John reached his destination quickly. At the door to the apartment, he put down the brown bag, finishing a mouthful of the baguette.

He tested the doorknob, not surprised in the least to find it locked.

Glancing up and down the hall, John checked to make sure no one else was around. Satisfied to see he was alone, he grasped the handle tightly and drove a shoulder into the door. Wood creaked and gave way with little protest to John's mass and strength, swinging open to reveal a dimly lit living room.

Light shone through the closed blinds in stripes, like an old detective noir film. John slipped into the apartment, picking up the grocery bag and swinging the door closed as far as it would go. He searched through the rooms quickly, looking for any clues that would link Keppler to the Four Serpents.

He powered up the computer on a small desk in one corner. While he waited, John rifled through the tidy stack of mail on the kitchen table. A few junk mail letters and a couple of bills, but not much else. He opened up the drawers, rummaging around for anything that would point him in the right direction.

After the cursory search turned up nothing useful, the computer's pleasant chime and the whirring fans got John's attention as the monitor flickered to life.

John clicked the mouse, and found a prompt screen, asking for a password to log in.

He cursed to himself for not letting Parker come with him to France. This obstacle would likely prove little challenge for the gifted programmer. He thought about calling and having Parker talk him through bypassing the screen, but decided it would take more time than he probably had.

John decided to dig a little deeper through all of the drawers in the apartment. Keppler kept his place neat and tidy. This was both good and bad for John, as it meant while it wouldn't take long to go through the available notes and other information, there just wouldn't be much for him to actually search through. After the desk drawers proved fruitless, John headed into the bedroom.

He tossed the contents of the two nightstand drawers onto the bed, but stopped while he held the second empty drawer in his hand. This one felt lighter than the first after he had dumped everything out. It was only a slight difference, but enough for John to notice. He put the drawer down and grabbed the first one. His hunch was correct, this one felt heavier. He turned it over in his hands and noticed that it was the slightest bit shallower inside as well.

With no time for subtlety, John smashed his fist through the bottom of the drawer. The thin false underside splintered revealing a leather bound black notebook wedged inside. John plucked the journal from the drawer and saw a small flash drive tucked next to it.

Mouth drawn in a straight line, he turned the drive over in his fingers. *No way to look at the files here.* He opened the notebook and saw notes and descriptions written in German, and cursed again. The only thing rustier than his French right now was his German.

John walked into the living room as he flipped through the pages, and heard two car doors close outside. He pushed the slats of the blinds apart with the notebook and looked out the window down to the street level. He saw a black sedan parked outside as two RAID agents headed inside the building.

All out of time, John thought. He exited the apartment, closing the broken door behind him, mostly out of habit, and headed for the stairs. It was clear to him that they were heading for Matthias' apartment. If he headed down the stairs, he would run into them.

John went down one floor and stepped out of the stairwell, into the hallway. He heard the sounds of footsteps coming up the stairs as he closed the door to the fourth-floor landing behind him.

The boot steps and voices of the two men passed by as they continued up the stairs, and into the hallway above. He had to move fast. Once they saw the busted door, they would realize immediately that someone was in there.

John slipped down the stairs as quietly as he could, heading out the front door into the street. He jogged around the corner of the building, then began to walk away at a leisurely pace, blending into the foot traffic in the neighborhood.

* * *

Lionel Gavreau and Christopher Brassard ascended the stairs leading to Dietrich Byrne's apartment, exiting into a dark hallway with faded carpet, worn thin where they stood. As they headed toward the front door, Gavreau held up a hand, halting the other man.

Brassard unholstered his Glock 17 and held it at low ready. Gavreau stepped to the door, examining splintered wood around the lock. He looked at Brassard, and nodded, then unholstered his own pistol, a 44 Magnum Smith & Wesson 629. He pushed the door open quietly, and Brassard slid into the room like a ghost.

Gavreau moved in right behind, and they cleared the small apartment, room by room, with practiced precision. Neither man spoke, but both knew exactly what the other was doing at all times.

"Clear," Brassard said.

"Clear," Gavreau responded.

Both men holstered their weapons. Gavreau shook his head in frustration, his hand absently reaching for his jaw again.

"Do you think it was Stone?" Brassard asked.

"Yes, I think it was," Gavreau said. He kicked the grocery bag on the floor.

"These groceries are fresh. I can still smell the bread," Gavreau said, examining the large bite taken out of the baguette.

Brassard let out a sigh. "One of the drawers in the bedroom is smashed apart. Maybe he found something hidden in there."

Gavreau walked the apartment, also noting how clean and tidy it was even after John's hasty search. He stopped in the living room.

"Grab that computer. Maybe we can find something that the American missed," Gavreau said.

"Yes sir," Brassard responded, and went to work, pulling the cables from the wall.

Stone was a thorn in his side once again. Gavreau tightened his jaw and let the pain serve to replace his frustration. He turned and swung a boot out hard, launching the chair at the computer desk across the living room.

"Is everything alright, sir?" Brassard stood with the computer tucked under his arm.

Gavreau waved his man off. "Once we find John Stone, I'm going to make sure we bury him with charges for interfering in our investigation. If the Four Serpents strike again, Stone will have blood on his hands."

* * *

Azhaar bin Hashim stood in a courtyard, admiring the French skyline. He didn't hate those that were not believers. His was a bigger mission, against a greater enemy. Those in the government that would control its citizens with their heathen ways, and no moral compass.

A giant of a man, bin Hashim's bodyguard, entered the courtyard. Kaliq followed close behind. Though the smaller man stood a full two heads shorter than the brute, he showed no fear, physically mimicking his movements and mannerisms.

They both stood, waiting for bin Hashim's command, Kaliq positioning himself and posturing like the guard. Bin Hashim smiled at the sight of the two then nodded to the larger man. The bodyguard turned to let Kaliq pass and frowned at the sight of the smaller man seeming to mock him.

That wasn't the case, however, and the guard was told as such. The head of the Four Serpents summoned this small, strange man personally. Kaliq possessed a high-level skill set that allowed him to infiltrate and complete tasks many others would find too difficult.

The trade-off was that he always seemed to behave in a peculiar way, imitating physical characteristics he would see in others. He spoke very little, and when he did, he would rarely stay on topic. Bin Hashim accepted his quirks and utilized Kaliq's ability to it's fullest to further their cause.

"Come in, my friend," bin Hashim said to the man.

Kaliq took two more steps forward then stopped. They stood in silence for a few awkwardly long moments, when bin Hashim decided to break the silence.

"The man, Matthias. Is he dead?" bin Hashim asked.

The assassin rocked side to side slightly and nodded.

"Matthias is Dietrich. Dietrich is dead."

Bin Hashim found the response somewhat confusing but smiled at the news. Kaliq's affirmative nod was all the answer the Serpent leader needed. His words would tend come out in short, often irrelevant sentences, all over the place at times, but physical movements were always the true intent of what Kaliq wanted to express.

"This is excellent news, friend," bin Hashim said, a genuine smile on his face.

Matthias fully funded the operation for The Four Serpents, with the promise of riches and power beyond anything he could imagine. His greed was his undoing, as it was for many westerners in power. The plan bin Hashim set into motion was the most ambitious idea of any jihad ever attempted. Years in the planning, costing so much money to implement, that outside sources were necessary to provide the required capital.

The tradeoff was the elevated risk of exposure, however. Once the pieces of bin Hashim's plan were in place, the Serpents systematically eliminated anyone involved that hadn't pledged one hundred percent loyalty to the organization. Matthias was the last variable, and with that final loose end tied off, they could now implement their plan in the shadows.

"Kaliq, my friend, it is time for you to begin the next step."

The assassin nodded. "The doctor. Get the doctor," he said.

CHAPTER

9

Los Angeles, California

Parker combed his fingers back through his hair, staring at the progress bar for his search. On the bed next to his desk, AC/DC's *Highway to Hell* started playing, the ringtone telling him right away who was calling. He tapped the button on his earpiece to answer the call.

"Hey John, how's everything going?" Parker asked.

"I could use a little help. I found a key drive, and I need to pull all the data. I'm just not able to get into it," John said.

"Sure thing buddy. Give me a sec," Parker said.

A few clicks on his keyboard, and the desktop screen of John's laptop computer appeared on Parker's monitor. Parker's eyes opened wide for a moment at the chaotic clutter of files and folders scattered all over the desktop.

"Ugh, your file structure is an abomination. Don't you use folders?" Parker asked.

"Sue me," John said.

"Are you still using the eight dot three naming convention? This is like staring at the nineties."

"Parker, please," John said. *"We don't have time to screw around."*

Parker chuckled and moved the cursor over the drive icon on the desktop, double-clicking it. A moment later, the security prompt opened on the window.

"Hmmm, let's see what we have here," Parker said.

Parker's fingers danced over the keyboard, sometimes pausing before resuming the staccato rhythm. The dual monitor setup allowed him to access his own computer files as well as those on John's computer.

"Your corporate *shelfware* is no match for my digital wizardry," he mumbled.

"What?"

"Oh. Nothing," Parker said. "I mean, ta-da." He flourished his hands, knowing John wouldn't be able to see the gesture.

The key drive icon opened to reveal a list of folders with cryptic names. Nothing stood out to Parker as he scanned through them. The arrow on

John's desktop began to move toward one of the folders. Parker chuckled imagining John being too impatient and opening the files on his own now.

The first folder opened, displaying a list of text files. Again, nothing stood out. One by one, John searched each of the folders on the drive, occasionally battling for control of the computer with Parker. The programmer finally relented, letting John take point.

"Looks like a bunch of text files," John said.

"Hang on, John," Parker said retaking control of John's computer. "Let me try something."

Parker copied the contents of the flash drive to his own computer.

"I cast *detect magic*," He said, running a subroutine that scanned through all the text files, looking for patterns, like recurring names and dates.

After a couple of minutes, the program started populating a growing list to display its findings.

"I see names listed here, with dates and Euro amounts. These look like payments between two parties. I mean it looks pretty innocuous, but given that it was in a secret drive—"

John made a sound like an impatient grunt, interrupting Parker's monologue.

"Right, sorry," Parker said.

Parker clicked a few keys and dragged a window around until John could see Parker's desktop displayed on his own laptop.

* * *

"Like I said, nothing out of the ordinary here, unless these are payments for some type of nefarious purpose," Parker said.

John sat at the desk of a new hotel room and scanned the names on the list. He looked for anyone linked to Matthias Keppler, or any of his known aliases.

"Parker, can you tell if any of the bank accounts listed here are somehow connected with more than one person on this list?" John asked.

"There isn't enough information," Parker said. *"All I've got are the last four digits of each account and in some cases the name of the bank."*

John sat back in his seat. "Why would Keppler have this information?"

"He's a middleman. A financier," Parker said.

John focused his attention on the recipients, scanning down the list until one near the middle grabbed his attention.

"Wait, C. Brassard. I recognize that name. He's one of the RAID guys. Gavreau's second in command," John said, sitting up straighter.

"*Hold on. I'll check him out,*" Parker said.

John saw windows opening and text flying across the view of Parker's desktop on his laptop. He was in awe of how fast Parker was moving and processing the information he found. A picture showed Christopher's Brassard's identification photo and career credentials.

"That's him," John said. "Get me everything you can about him."

"*You think he's dirty?*" Parker asked. "*I mean, what if RAID is using him as an undercover agent to infiltrate the Four Serpents?*"

"Under his real name? Do it, Parker. We can't take any chances."

CHAPTER
10

RAID HQ

The RAID team computer tech finished hooking up Matthias Keppler's computer and powering it up.

"How old is this thing?" Brassard asked as several minutes passed.

After several more diagnostic screens flashed, the operating system started, greeting the team with the login prompt.

"Okay, it might be a while before I can get in here," the tech said.

"How long?" Gavreau asked.

"Well, if we could guess his password, not long at all. Did you happen to find any clues that would point us in the right direction?"

Gavreau grew impatient. "No, nothing. Just do what you can to get in there."

"Alright. It might be a while," the tech said, repeating himself.

The man rolled his chair to another computer and pulled up a command prompt screen.

"I'll be back," Brassard said.

Gavreau grunted his acknowledgment, staying focused on the tech and Keppler's computer.

Brassard exited the room and made his way to the stairwell. He took the stairs instead of the elevator, heading for the blind spot he knew about in the building's security camera coverage. Once out from under the digital eye of the surveillance system, he pulled a SIM card from a hidden pocket and swapped the one in his cell phone.

Brassard continued down to the front exit of the building. He walked outside and down the street, to a nearby bench. Once there, he sat down and lit up a cigarette before sending a message on his phone, attaching the digital files he had on John Stone.

Brassard casually finished his cigarette, grinding the butt out with his boot, and walked back into the RAID headquarters.

He went up the stairs, switching his SIM card out in the same blind spot, and headed back to the IT room. Gavreau exited the door as he opened it, so Brassard followed the commander.

"It's going to be a while," Gavreau said, the frustration in his voice evident.

"Is there anything you need now?" Brassard asked.

"No, thank you. I'll be in my office. Call me if the techs find anything."

"Yes, sir."

Brassard watched the RAID commander head into his office, closing the door behind him. He then headed into the room with the computer tech.

* * *

Omari Malouf groaned as he sat on the floor next to his children. The smile on his face beamed, made brighter by the wonderful scent wafting out from the kitchen where his wife prepared their supper. Omari's son and daughter laughed and rolled around as he joined them.

"What are we playing now?" he asked.

His five-year-old son jumped on Omari's back as he leaned over to tickle his daughter.

"You're a horsey, now!" his son squealed.

He laughed as he caught his breath for a moment, then began to crawl around the living room, whinnying and neighing. Omari's daughter, only three and a half, started to walk in front of him holding an imaginary treat to lead him.

"Carrot. Want carrot?" she asked.

81

He followed her around for a bit, then without warning, rose up waving his hands in the air, like a horse standing on its hind legs. His son screamed, and wrapped his arms around his father's neck, squealing with laughter.

A cell phone on the end table buzzed. Omari trotted like a horse on his hands and knees, taking his son to the couch.

"Okay, son, horsey needs a break," he said, bucking his son onto the couch.

"Me too!" his daughter said.

Chuckling, he swung his daughter onto his back, then bucked her off gently onto the couch next to her brother. Omari stood and picked up his phone. His smile faltered slightly as he read the incoming message. He spoke to his son, careful not to let his smile change now.

"Take your sister to your room, and play until dinner is ready."

"Yes, daddy," his son said. He grabbed his sister's hand and led her down the hall.

Omari read the message from his contact in RAID, frowning when he saw that they found out about Matthias, securing a computer from his residence. He skimmed over the information about the American, John Stone. Would this man be a threat to the upcoming plans?

He closed the message then dialed a number on his phone. After two rings, someone on the other end answered.

"It's Omari. I need to speak with him," he said.

"We will call you back." Before Omari could say anything, the line disconnected.

He sat on the couch and waited for a few agonizing minutes. The ringing phone startled Omari, snapping him out of his haze. He knew that the line would be secured on the other end.

"What do you want?" Azhaar bin Hashim asked.

"There is a complication with Matthias. RAID has taken the computer from his apartment," Omari said.

"Are you positive?"

"Yes. Our contact has confirmed."

Bin Hashim sighed on the other end, then silence. Omari wiped a bead of sweat from his brow, wanting to say something, anything, to break the silence. He feared it was a judgment of his fate for this news.

"Very well. We will have to move up the timetable, now," bin Hashim said. *"Get your part ready, Malouf. Do not fail me in this mission."*

"It will be done," Omari answered.

* * *

Minutes stretched out, feeling like hours before Parker sighed over the speakerphone.

"There is no evidence of wrongdoing that can be pinned on this Brassard guy," He said.

"You can't find anything connecting Brassard and Keppler?" John asked.

"I found records of money transferred to his account, which is innocuous enough since I don't know who sent the payments. But, given the size of the transfers and Matthias' dubious nature—"*

"I have to tell Gavreau," John said, interrupting.

" Tell him what? We don't have much here."

"This is too much of a coincidence. We can't risk having a rat in that task force," John answered.

"We?"

"Now isn't the time to worry about jurisdictions," John said. "The Four Serpents are still out there. They could strike again at any time, and right now RAID could be compromised."

"Yeah, I guess you're right," Parker said.

John pulled the small USB key drive from his laptop, stuffed it into a pocket, and grabbed Keppler's leather-bound notebook.

"See if you can find anything that could tell me where to go next," John said.

"I'll see what I can do, but Keppler was just a money man. I'm not sure I'll find any specific evidence," Parker said.

"Run the rest of the team, Parker. Make sure there are no other surprises."

"The entire team?" Parker asked.

"Yes. Especially Gavreau," John said before ending the call and heading out the door.

CHAPTER
11

RAID HQ, France

It was past 8pm, and the most of the personnel in the office had already gone home. Gavreau spent most of the afternoon and early evening at his desk, or in the computer rooms, bothering the techs handling Keppler's computer. He finally stood up from his chair and stretched before turning out the lights and closing his door as he left the office.

"Goodnight, Diana," he said as he passed the reception desk.

"Good night, sir," she replied.

Gavreau headed for the parking lot, pulling the keys from his pocket to unlock his car. He reached for the handle to the driver side door, when someone spoke behind him.

"We need to talk." The deep voice came from the shadows.

Gavreau turned to look, pivoting with his feet, to square up with the voice behind him. A head turn alone would leave him vulnerable. The American, John Stone, stepped into the golden glow from an overhead light.

In one smooth motion, Gavreau had his Smith & Wesson 629 drawn from the holster, its sights centered on the American's chest.

John's hands rose up to shoulder height, palms forward to show he was unarmed. "Easy, I come in peace," he said.

"You are under arrest, Stone. Keep your hands up," Gavreau said.

The two men stared at each other in a tense stand-off. John waiting to see what Gavreau would do next, and The RAID commander playing out the possibilities of John resisting arrest in his head.

It was John that broke the silent tension.

"I have information you need, that's bigger than this," John said, gesturing to the pistol in Gavreau's hand.

"You can tell me everything you need to when we're back inside the headquarters," Gavreau said, reaching for his radio with his free hand.

"It's about Brassard," John said looking him in the eye.

Gavreau froze. His grip on the pistol tightened, and he stared daggers at the American.

"What did you do to Christopher?" he asked, venom dripping from his words.

"He's fine," John said to assure Gavreau. "But I think he's been compromised."

"Do not dare to question my men," he said through gritted teeth.

"I have something to show you," John said.

Though he was not as muscular as John, Gavreau was just as tall. The tension permeated the space between the two, a near tangible presence.

"You have 10 seconds to convince me, Stone." Gavreau's hand lowered from his radio.

"Brassard has been receiving payments from someone. Matthias Keppler was handling the transfers," John said.

"I hope you do not think baseless accusations are going to sway me," the RAID commander said. His anger made his French accent thicker.

John nodded and moved one hand slowly toward his pocket. Gavreau's pistol remained firmly aimed at John. He pulled the key drive from his pocket and tossed it casually toward the RAID commander.

Gavreau caught it with his free hand, the heavy revolver never wavering.

"What is on this?" he asked, holding up the drive, eyes still fixed on John.

"I got it from the apartment of Dietrich Byrne. That was just one of Matthias Keppler's many aliases. Those files are Keppler's financial records," John said. "Brassard's name is in there. Multiple times. I think he's been working for someone else for a while now. I'm sorry, Gavreau."

"How do I know you are telling the truth?" Gavreau asked.

"I didn't have to come find you, but this was too important to let go."

Gavreau paused, then nodded slightly.

John pulled the notebook from his back pocket and held it out. "I found this with the drive. I don't speak German, so it's no good to me. Maybe it will help your investigation."

"Okay, I will look at them. Give me your number, and the address where you're staying, and I will get in contact with you," Gavreau said.

"With all due respect, I'd rather not. I'll get in touch with you later," John said.

John figured they would know the first hotel he was staying in after the hospital incident. He had to move and didn't want them to know which hotel he had chosen after that.

Gavreau raised his 44 Magnum for a second, contemplating just arresting Stone on the spot. John remained calm throughout the entire encounter. He finally relented and lowered the revolver. Gavreau gave him a short nod, and John backed away into the shadows. He holstered his pistol and turned the key drive over in his fingers.

"Chris. Please don't let this be true," Gavreau said to himself.

CHAPTER

12

John sat in a window seat in the train, traveling from Lyon to his hotel. The lights of the city flashed by, lulling him into a trance. He needed rest, and this would be an excellent time to catch up. But his meditation was disrupted by his phone ringing. He saw Parker's number, figuring he was calling with updates to his research.

"Parker, what's up?" John asked.

"John, I checked out Gavreau and his team. They're clean, at least where Keppler's ledger is concerned."

"That's good enough for now. I gave Keppler's files to Gavreau," John said.

"There's something else on those files. It might be a clue to what the Four Serpents are planning," Parker said.

"What is it?"

"I looked up all the names in the ledger, and most of them are people suspected of terrorism, or on some type of watch list. One of them stood out. Jean-Paul Rolland. This ledger you

found will go a long way to help shine a light on some pretty bad guys. This guy stuck out as different, though. He's not the type normally—"

"Parker, please. Get to the point," John interrupted.

"Oh right, sorry." The programmer was brilliant at his work but had a tendency to ramble when excited.

"Yeah, anyway, this man, Rolland, set up an annual convention, the Science Summit on global warming. You're not going to believe your luck, John. It's happening in Paris, right now," Parker said.

"What do the Serpents want with Rolland?" John asked.

"I looked closely at his background and nothing jumped out," Parker said. *"So, next I pulled up a list of the people presenting their research there. I cross-referenced the names with their respective fields, and one raised some red flags. I figured you might agree that this has to be more than just coincidence."*

John sat up straight shaking the sleep out of his head.

"Dr. Steven Takada is a scientist and engineer from San Fransisco. He's going be there giving a talk about weather patterns, and climate change caused by catastrophic events. The presentation is about using global weather satellites to increase the accuracy of predicting storms."

"Parker, you're straying off topic again. How does that raise any red—"

Parker continued. *"Trust me, John, I haven't strayed. The thing is, Takada's isn't a climatologist. His latest research has been on the development of kinetic weapon technology,"* Parker said.

"What is that, exactly?" John asked.

"Are you familiar with the Lazy Dogs from the Vietnam war?" Parker asked.

"I've heard a little. The US military dropped thousands of solid steel slugs from a high altitude onto hidden targets under soft cover."

"Yes, that's it. The theory was that the slugs, about 2 to 3 inches long, would generate terminal velocity when dropped from high enough. The mass of the projectiles would be able to penetrate deep into the ground, into the tunnel systems used by the Viet Cong. Now imagine that weapon system, but scaled up," Parker said.

"How big are we talking?" John asked.

"Right now Dr. Takada's projectiles are about ten times larger. Approximately two and a half foot tungsten-rich rods, optimized for striking at longer ranges. The delivery system is an unmanned aerial vehicle. The UAVs are capable of carrying about a dozen of these bad boys," Parker said.

"What type of damage are we talking?" John asked.

"A single rod alone would be devastating. It could bring down a five-story building, at least. It's a weaponized meteor

strike. A dozen of them, patterned just right…" Parker said, letting his statement trail off.

John let out a long sigh. The Serpents paid Jean-Paul Rolland, which meant they must have some inside knowledge of the summit, including Dr. Takada's presence. Parker was right, this couldn't be a mere coincidence.

"Do you know how far along his research is?" John asked.

"The formulas and calculations are complete. Right down to the level of accuracy, and destructive force. As far as the development of the physical weapon system, I don't know."

John had to assume at least a prototype of the system could be close to completion. The Four Serpents might be going to kidnap the doctor and force him to finish the weapon for them. That was a scenario that he couldn't let that happen. If they had even one of those rods, the results would be catastrophic, but if they had the ability to make and deploy more, the level of global terror would shift dramatically.

"I have to get to that summit. I can't let the Serpents get to Takada." John said.

"Should we warn Gavreau?" Parker asked.

John thought about it for a moment. "No, he's gonna have his hands full dealing with the corruption

94

in his team. Besides, I'm not sure I want him knowing what I'm going to do. He might try to stop me."

"This is getting way out of hand, John. You can't do this by yourself," Parker said.

"Parker, if I can grab Takada before the Serpents do, I can end all of this."

The train slowed to a stop at the station near his hotel.

"I have to go. Send me everything you have on Dr. Takada, and the summit," John said.

Parker sighed and paused, contemplating trying to talk some sense into his friend, but he knew it was no use. *"Will do, John."*

John stepped off the train and walked quickly to his hotel. He would have to get to Paris as soon as he could. Time was running out.

* * *

Orsay, France

Lionel Gavreau sat at the desk of the small office in his home. He held the flash drive in his hand, staring at it. John Stone gave him the notebook and drive before dropping a heavy accusation against Christopher Brassard. One of Gavreau's own. RAID was like a family to him, and Brassard was a brother.

Who was Stone, to accuse his brother of treason? He thought about smashing the device on the spot, pressing his thumb firmly against the plastic case. This could be a trick, used to delay him from coming after John to arrest him.

Then why would he meet me alone? Gavreau thought. To make the trap more believable?

He fought against the doubt and uncertainty, finally inserting the drive into the data slot on his computer. His body stiffened, prepared for whatever would show up.

The device opened automatically when inserted, a subroutine on the drive seemingly bypassing the login window that popped up. Gavreau stared at the directory of folders within. This was the information John found at Keppler's apartment.

One file opened itself, and Gavreau let out a shocked breath when he saw the contents. It was a list of money transfers Keppler had arranged, all sent to Christopher Brassard. The dates of the transactions went back years.

Gavreau clenched his fists. He wanted to smash his monitor and make the damning evidence disappear. This wasn't possible. Rage flooded through him. At Chris' betrayal. At John for this trick, to cause him to doubt his team, his family. Because the American revealed evidence of something happening under Gavreau's nose for all these years. He closed his eyes tight, squeezing tears free.

After several deep, shaky breaths, Gavreau regained his composure and opened his eyes, forcing himself to read everything Stone wanted him to see. His vision blurred from the tears. He wiped them away and kept reading. His blood boiled, filling him with a desire for justice, or vengeance.

When he read through all the files, Gavreau yanked the device from his computer, scooped up the notebook, and walked out of his house.

* * *

Somewhere in Europe

Curtis Clarke snapped awake, pulled from his slumber by the rattling buzz of his cell phone. He checked the clock as he reached for his phone. He'd only been asleep for a couple of hours and fought to clear his head.

"Hello?" He said, stifling a yawn and trying to sound alert.

"Curtis, it's Parker Lewis," the voice on the other end said.

Curtis sat up, turning to put his feet on the rough carpet. "Parker, what's going on?"

He hadn't been in contact with Parker Lewis for months. Hearing from him now caught him off guard. They hadn't had any contact since Congress dismantled the Hostile Response Division.

"It's John. I think he needs some help," Parker said.

"Stone? Is he okay?"

Another name from the HRD. This one much more notorious than Parker. Before the end of the HRD, John Stone had been accused of acts of domestic terrorism and treason. The task to bring him into custody fell squarely on Curtis' shoulders. He ultimately let John go, when push came to shove, and Stone eventually proved the charges against him had been fabricated.

Though some tension still remained between the two, Curtis and John parted on amicable terms. Now, out of the blue, Curtis' past came storming back into his life.

CHAPTER
13

Paris, France

Christopher Brassard sat back on the couch, taking another sip of his beer while watching TV and winding down. The doorbell barged in on his relaxation as he sat up, turning the volume down. He walked to the door and saw Gavreau though the small window as he got closer.

"Good evening, Lionel. What brings you here at this time of night?" Chris asked.

"Hi Chris, sorry to come by so late," Lionel said.

"Nonsense, my friend. Come on in."

The smile on Gavreau's face twitched and faltered before returning.

"So, what can I do for you?" Chris asked.

Gavreau paused for a long moment, then looked Brassard in the eye.

"You can tell me. Tell me how long you've been selling secrets to the enemy. How long you've put money over the lives of your own family."

"Wh-what are you talking about?" Brassard asked with a confused and lopsided grin.

Gavreau reached out, grasping the front of Chris' t-shirt. His fist shot out like a piston, across the man's jaw. Gavreau released his grip, letting Brassard crumple to the ground.

"What the hell is wrong with you?" Brassard yelled from the floor, wiping a hand across his bloodied mouth.

"A rat! You're a rat, selling out your brothers and sisters to the Four Serpents!"

Brassard backed away, scrambling to his feet. "I don't even know what you're talking about!"

Gavreau produced the key drive, pointing it accusingly at Brassard's chest.

"I have the records. Money transfers going back years! How could you do this?"

Brassard stammered, unable to put a coherent argument together. He held his hands out as if he were warding away the evidence on the flash drive. His mouth opened and closed, looking for the right response.

"I-I can explain, man. It's not what you think—" Brassard started.

"You can explain it to the rest of the team at HQ. Let's go," Gavreau interrupted.

He snatched Brassard by the back of his neck and roughly shoved him to the front door. His second-in-command did not try to resist.

"Okay. Just give me a second to grab my keys," Brassard said.

"Don't bother. I'm driving," Gavreau said.

Brassard nodded but continued walking toward the table in the hallway, where his keys were sitting. Gavreau grabbed him by the shoulder to spin him around.

"I said I'm—"

Brassard used the momentum to lash out with his elbow, catching Gavreau across the temple. The RAID commander staggered back, dazed. He saw Brassard dash for the hallway table, and reach under it. A secret compartment dropped away from the bottom, revealing a small black pistol inside.

Gavreau lunged forward, trying to reach Brassard before he grabbed the gun. He was a heartbeat too slow. Brassard wheeled around to face him. Gavreau hoped the man would extend his shooting arm in a panic to fire, allowing him to control the arm with the pistol and close the distance.

He had no such luck, however. Like the rest of Gavreau's team, Brassard was highly trained and not

101

easily shaken. He spun using his free hand to post the commander back while keeping his pistol hand tight inside to fire from his waist.

Gavreau pivoted as the pistol cracked, the round grazing a rib. Pain flashed through Gavreau's mind, and he fought to stay focused. He pinned Brassard's free arm against his body and shoved him into the table. Gavreau whipped a heavy hook into the man's kidney.

His fist dug in deep, rewarding him with a grunt and hiss through Brassard's clenched teeth. He followed with a high hook catching Brassard just below the ear, on his jaw.

Brassard struggled to pull away, and Gavreau grabbed the pistol with a firm grip, keeping the barrel pointed away. They wrestled for a moment, and the handgun fired again. Pain and heat caused Gavreau to release his grip.

The momentary lapse allowed Brassard to spin and backpedal to create distance between the two. He grasped his pistol in a two-handed grip and pressed the trigger, the sights aimed in the center of Gavreau's chest.

Click

Brassard's eyes widened at the malfunction, but his reflexes took over, allowing him to quickly go through the motions to clear the weapon.

The RAID commander was ready for that misfire, however. He was holding the slide of the pistol when it fired the second time, so he knew the weapon wouldn't have ejected the brass and chambered the next round. He moved forward when Brassard tried to shoot, making no attempt to evade.

Gavreau closed the distance and grasped the weapon with both of his hands. With an animalistic growl, he yanked the pistol toward him and cracked Brassard in the face with a headbutt. With a quick twist, Gavreau wrenched the gun free. Brassard buried a front kick, deep into Gavreau's stomach, sending him reeling back.

He charged the RAID commander, reaching for the pistol. Lionel allowed him to get close, feinting a retreat. At the last moment, he pivoted and executed a perfect shoulder throw. Brassard sailed over his body, crashing through the coffee table, onto the hardwood floor.

The wind exploded from Brassard's lungs violently, sending out a spray of spittle and blood. Gavreau followed up with a straight left across the man's jaw, leaving him in a heap on the floor. Lionel cleared and emptied the pistol and stuck it into his waistband. Then he pulled a pair of handcuffs from his pocket and secured them tightly to Brassard's wrists.

"Get up!" He yanked the man up by the wrists.

Brassard let out a groan and wheeze, as he stumbled out the front door, to Gavreau's waiting car.

CHAPTER
14

Bièvres, Essonne - RAID Headquarters

"What's all this about?" Lussier asked.

William Silvestre, Giles Deschanel, and Alban Lussier stood in the lobby of the RAID headquarters. Gavreau called them, issuing orders to come in right away for an emergency meeting.

"Beats me. I was asleep when the commander called," Silvestre said.

"Should we gear up?" Deschanel asked. "We're probably about to hit the Four Serpents."

They saw a pair of headlights aiming right for the front entrance. All three men tensed for a moment. The parking lot was on the side of the building, so a car pulling up to the front was highly unusual.

The car stopped, and the headlights turned off. The three members headed outside when they heard the car door opening. When they got outside, they saw Gavreau, pulling a battered and bleeding Christopher Brassard from the other side.

The second-in-command was in handcuffs and looking down.

"What the hell is this? Uh, sir." Deschanel asked.

Gavreau didn't say a word as he shoved Brassard into the building's front entrance. Christopher fell to his knees, and Gavreau yanked him back to his feet.

"This, rat, sold his soul for his own personal gain. Put us all at risk," Gavreau finally said.

"What are you talking about?" Lussier asked.

The three men looked at Brassard, who kept his eyes on the floor and said nothing. Gavreau pulled a key drive out of his pocket and tossed it to Silvestre.

"There are files on that drive. They show money transfers to Brassard, arranged by Matthias Keppler. The financier who worked with bin Hashim and the Four Serpents."

All three men looked at Gavreau, then Brassard, with shocked expressions.

"That's not true—" Brassard began. Gavreau shoved him forward, almost throwing him to the floor.

"Shut your mouth!" he spat. "You'll have plenty of time to tell us everything in interrogation."

Silvestre stared at the flash drive in his hand. Deschanel got his attention as Gavreau led Brassard away.

"Do you think it's true?" Deschanel asked.

Silvestre shrugged.

"Open the drive. We have to see for ourselves," Lussier said.

Silvestre hesitated, turning the drive over between his thumb and forefinger. "I can't believe this. How can it be true? It can't be."

Lussier reached over and gently grasped the key drive. Silvestre held on for a second, contemplating whether to even let anyone open it. Brassard was like a brother to him. He had even saved Silvestre's life two years ago, when an operation hit an unexpected level of armed resistance.

After a few seconds, Silvestre looked Lussier in the eye and released his grip, letting him have the drive. Gavreau had already taken Brassard toward the elevator and pressed the button to head to interrogation. Lussier, Deschanel, and Silvestre followed solemnly behind them.

On the third floor, the doors opened, and they all filed out. Gavreau had a hand on Brassard's shoulder, guiding him to a holding cell. Lussier took the drive to his desk and powered up his computer. The three men stood and waited for what seemed like an eternity for the computer to boot up.

When the log in screen finally showed, Lussier logged in with his credentials and inserted the key drive into the data port. The files opened, showing them precisely what Gavreau had seen.

It was true. Everything Gavreau told them. Christopher Brassard betrayed all of them.

* * *

Gavreau opened the door to the holding cell, leading Brassard inside. Resigned to his fate, he sat quietly on the hard bench against the back wall. Gavreau stood and regarded his colleague. Could he even consider him a colleague? Was he ever one of them?

They remained motionless for a few tense minutes, Brassard choosing silence, and Gavreau left speechless. Silvestre walked over to the holding cell and looked at Brassard.

"How long?" Silvestre asked.

Brassard would not meet his gaze.

"Answer me! I—we, we all trusted you! We're a family!" Silvestre was screaming now.

Deschanel tried to calm his friend down, putting his reassuring hands on his shoulders. Lussier sat at his computer, poring over all the data on the key drive.

Gavreau finally turned and headed back out the exit, and closed the holding cell door. He walked to Lussier's desk, and the other two men followed him. There was a long silence, no one knew what to say first.

"How did you find this?" Deschanel asked.

"The American, John Stone. He was here earlier tonight, and he gave it to me," Gavreau said gesturing to the flash drive.

"The American? Can we trust this? Can we even trust him?" Silvestre asked, wishing none of this was true.

"Can we afford not to act on it?" Gavreau asked.

"Yes, we can. What if Stone gave you this to distract you from whatever he's planning?" Silvestre asked.

"You think Stone might be working for the Serpents? Creating a rift in this department?" Deschanel asked.

"You're grasping at straws now,' Gavreau answered.

"Can we believe him more than our own brother?" Silvestre chimed in.

"Brassard... Christopher tried to kill me," Gavreau said.

This left the three men in stunned silence.

"When I saw the files, I went right to his house. I called you all to meet me here, where we could get to the bottom of this," Gavreau started. The others stood and listened intently.

"When I saw Chris acting so natural, like he was one of us, I lost my temper. I punched him and told him we were coming here. Then he caught me with an elbow and went for a pistol," Gavreau gestured to his side, wincing slightly. The adrenaline was finally starting to wear off. The three men finally noticed the blood stain on his dark shirt.

"I got the pistol away from him and cuffed him. Then we came straight here."

Silvestre shook his head, not wanting to believe any of it. "Y-you hit him first. You said that yourself. Maybe he was defending himself."

"Stop. Just stop,'"Lussier finally said to Silvestre. "The evidence is all here. Brassard is dirty."

Silvestre grasped his own hair in two handfuls and let out a frustrated scream through clenched teeth. He turned and stormed away. Deschanel turned to follow him.

"It's okay. Let him have some time alone," Gavreau said.

The other two looked at each other, then at their task force commander.

"What do we do now?" Lussier asked.

Gavreau was silent for a long beat. He looked at the holding cell door.

"Interrogation," he said. "We need to find out what he's told the Serpents. What they know about us."

CHAPTER
15

Gavreau stood in the darkroom, looking through the two-way mirror, into the interrogation room. At a steel table, with his hands cuffed to the cold metal slab, Chris Brassard sat quietly. Patrice Cartier, The RAID lead interrogator, sat in the seat in front of him. Cartier asked another question, while Brassard sat in stony silence. William Silvestre stepped into the observation room, followed by Giles Deschanel.

Silvestre was more composed now than he was after learning about Brassard.

"Anything yet?" Deschanel asked.

"Nothing. Brassard hasn't said more than a handful of words up to this point," Gavreau answered.

"Look, I'm sorry I accused you earlier about—" Silvestre said.

"Forget it, Will. I understand how you feel. I didn't want it to be true either," Gavreau said.

"Chris was family to all of us," Deschanel said.

Silvestre just looked through the window at Brassard. Unable to find the words, he could only nod at the two of them.

"Why don't you go see how Lussier is doing with the files that Stone gave us, Will," Gavreau said.

"Sir," Silvestre said with a nod, turning to leave.

The interrogator, Cartier, stood and stepped out of the interrogation room. Brassard gave the slightest turn of his head toward the mirror, then returned his gaze straight ahead. Gavreau tightened his fists and shook his head. A few seconds later, the observation room door opened.

"He just will not speak with me," Cartier said, entering.

"The man is highly trained. Not the typical people we usually break down," Gavreau said.

"What do we do now?" Deschanel asked.

Cartier pushed his glasses up the bridge of his nose with a finger. "Well, my recommendation is to take him to a secure detention facility. There, we have better equipment and personnel to conduct things more efficiently."

"Torture? Are you kidding?" Deschanel asked, more to Gavreau than Cartier. The RAID commander held out a hand to reassure him.

"No one's going to any *black site*, Deschanel. Besides, we don't have time to waste sending him away from here," Gavreau said.

"Well, alright. It was just my recommendation, based on our need to prevent the next terrorist act the Four Serpents may be planning," Cartier said. "I can try to speak to him again, after he's had some time alone."

"Perhaps I could speak to him," Gavreau offered.

"I don't think that would be the best idea. The isolation will help when I interrogate him again later. Any aggravation may erase any progress we make," Cartier said.

Gavreau nodded. Cartier returned the nod before leaving. Gavreau and Deschanel stayed behind, watching Brassard through the glass.

"You're going in there, aren't you?" Deschanel asked.

"Yes," was all Gavreau said, then he left the room.

* * *

The bright overhead LED lights bathed the interrogation room in a cold, clinical glow. Brassard sat unmoving in his seat, waiting for the next round with Cartier. The interrogator was good, but he would get nothing from the former RAID operative.

The handle on the door rattled and turned, swinging open. Lionel Gavreau stepped through, locking his gaze right away. Brassard's eyes widened slightly, but otherwise, his expression betrayed nothing. Gavreau's were fixed intently on Brassard, as he pulled the chair out and sat down in the seat Cartier occupied earlier.

"I don't know what to say, *friend*," Gavreau said, biting the last word bitterly. "Were we even friends?"

Chris Brassard continued to stare blankly, saying nothing as he took in a deep breath, in and out through his nose. Gavreau wanted to reach across the table and throttle him. Make him feel the anger, sadness, and frustration he and the rest of his team felt right now.

"Why? That's all I want to know. After all, we've been through, you owe me at least that. You owe your brothers and sisters out there that much," Gavreau said.

Silence.

The lack of response left Gavreau exasperated. He looked at the table's scratched and marred metal surface, waiting, hoping Brassard would say anything.

"It's no use. I guess you were never loyal to the team. Well, you had us all fooled, while you just sold your family to collect a few pieces of silver. Maybe your loyalty only lies with money."

Gavreau stood to leave when Brassard spoke.

"Loyalty?" His tone equal parts pain and mockery.

Gavreau turned to face him.

"You question my loyalty when you should really question your morality," Brassard said.

"What is that supposed to mean?" Gavreau asked. "We save lives every day."

"Save lives?" Brassard furrowed his brow. "You paint a picture of us as a big happy family, as if that's something to be proud of. We call each other *brother*, then we smile like the *good guys* while we put our boots on the necks of the ones the government says are the *bad guys*."

He looked up at Gavreau now, a fire in his eyes.

"Things are about to change. The corruption of the powers that be is going to end when true justice rains down on them from on high. Spears from the heavens."

Gavreau felt a chill shoot through his body. The conviction in Brassard's words shook him. Had he ever really known this man in front of him.

"Christopher, please. Tell me what the Four Serpents are planning. Don't let the terrorists spill any more innocent blood."

"Those who sit idly by, while the corrupt rule over them aren't truly innocent, *brother*." Brassard spit the last word like it was a dagger into the heart of his former commander. "They deserve the same judgment as those that rule over them."

CHAPTER
16

Paris, France

Kaliq stepped out of the black SUV, tugging at his collar as he twisted and kinked his head side to side. One of bin Hashim's lieutenants put a hand on the assassin's shoulder.

"Easy, friend," he said, undoing the top button and loosening the tie. "You won't have to wear this much longer, but if you keep fidgeting around, they will suspect that we don't belong."

With his discomfort abated, Kaliq smiled and grunted a quick thanks. Four more Serpents followed the pair inside, walking to the metal detector set up at the main entrance. The security guard waved them through, staring at the indicator lights.

Each man, in turn, enters the building with no warning sirens from the checkpoint. As they strode further into the building, shoes echoing in the spacious hall, A man in a suit joined them.

"I'm Omari Malouf." He placed his right hand over his heart and gave the men a slight bow. "Here in service to Azhaar bin Hashim and the Four Serpents. Right this way."

He led them down the main hall to a side office, away from the crowds finding their seats in the main presentation hall. Omari opened the door and gestured for the men to enter, following after the last man.

Kaliq's eyes continued roving around the room, bouncing from wall to wall, corner to corner, taking everything in. He fixed his attention on a pair of black hard-shell cases, typically used to transport equipment for rock concerts. They were approximately 3 and a half feet long and lay sideways on the floor.

Omari unlocked one of the cases and opened it, stepping to the side. One of the Serpents approached and crouched down to examine the contents. There were large boxes and items filled with lighting and sound equipment for the presentations at the summit.

The crouched man nodded to another Serpent, then reached down to one end of the box. The other Serpent did the same, grasping a small handle inside the case on the other side. They both lifted out the stage equipment out on a long shelf. Omari smiled as the Serpents stared into the empty black interior of the crate.

He reached into the box and lifted out the false bottom, revealing the arsenal inside. Small automatic weapons and fully loaded magazines tucked into foam inserts to keep them from moving around during transport. Bin Hashim's lieutenant nodded, and the men went to work opening the second case.

* * *

At the main entrance of the Paris Convention Centere, John melted into the crowd waiting to enter. He looked at the hastily erected metal detectors, an apparent response to the terrorist attack in Lyon.

He wasn't exactly sure where he needed to go in this massive space, so he followed the general flow of the people walking in, who had a better idea of where they wanted to be. He looked down at the pass that Parker had him print out, but the seat and row number didn't tell him where to find Dr. Steven Takada.

After passing the security checkpoint, John smiled and retrieved his pass, stuffing it in the breast pocket of his jacket. Following the crowd, he saw the signage plastered all over for the summit. *I need to find a schedule where the speakers will present their research,* he thought.

The people around him hurried toward the main hall where the opening presentation would be starting. John stepped to the side and looked for Takada's name listed at one of the information kiosks. He would be speaking in half an hour in one of the larger rooms.

John hurried, now. He needed to reach the doctor and intercept him before the Four Serpents arrived to take him.

* * *

The Serpents each slung their loaded Skorpion sub-machine guns under their arms, hidden by their jackets. The lieutenant ordered his four men to join the rest of the attendees in one of the secondary halls for Dr. Takada's presentation.

"Come with me, Kaliq."

The assassin nodded and followed as they slipped out through a different door, toward the preparation rooms for the presenters.

* * *

John walked through the back corridors, passing several stage crew members, and presenters. He reached the back of the hall where Dr. Takada would be discussing his research with the other scientists in attendance. John looked at his watch. Twenty minutes until it would start.

John poked his head through the side entrance, scanning the stage and seating area, hoping to find the doctor already there, which would make his job a little easier. No such luck. The large conference area with high ceilings, commonly used for accommodating large structures and lighting setups, was still mostly empty.

Rows of stackable chairs had been set out for the presentation, and only a few of the seats were already filled. Most of the people were still in the main hall where the opening presentation had started minutes earlier.

John strode out toward the raised impromptu stage area with the lectern set up in the middle. Behind the podium was a large white screen for a projector. He composed himself with the confidence of someone that was supposed to be there, looking around for a back entrance from where Dr. Takada would enter.

He stepped onto the stage area and headed for the back off to one side. There he found a small set of steps leading to an entrance blocked from the front of the room by a curtain.

John opened the door stepped into an adjoining smaller conference room area. Inside people were preparing to give their own presentations throughout the day. They sat at the various tables spread around the room, fiddling with a variety of props and equipment stacked on them.

In one corner, John spotted Dr. Takada holding a stack of index cards. He was reading through them, going over his presentation, unaware that his life was in jeopardy.

John made his way to the doctor as casually as he could, but without hesitation. He stopped two tables away from Takada and examined the unattended items on display, pretending to be there for that reason.

He angled himself in a way that allowed him to see much of the room, but still, keep an eye on the doctor. Another man joined Takada, speaking to him after he finished going over his notes. John overheard them discussing the plan and timing of the presentation.

Once their conversation ended, the other man left Dr. Takada alone. John approached him, speaking in a calm but authoritative tone.

"Doctor Takada?" he asked.

"Yes, what is it?" the doctor answered without looking up from a piece of equipment he was examining.

"Doctor, I need you to come with me, please." John spoke as if he were coordinating the events, trying to get Takada to blindly obey.

"What for?" Takada asked. He finally looked up and paused for a moment at the size of John.

"I just need to go over the slide deck for your presentation today. If you please," John said, beginning to walk toward the entrance to the stage.

It worked. Takada smiled, adjusted something on his equipment, and followed him. Now that the doctor was compliant, John needed to get him out through another exit, before anyone spotted them. He angled slightly, moving toward the backstage area.

"Actually, it's this way, sorry," John said as he redirected the doctor.

Takada followed the course change but seemed confused.

"What's out there? I thought my equipment was already set up." He said.

Without breaking his stride, John looked back and gave the doctor a nod and a smile. He led the unsuspecting man out the door, into another hall, this one narrow and empty. John dropped the ruse once they were alone.

"Dr. Takada, I don't want to alarm you, but I need to get you out of here for your safety."

Takada's expression switched from genuine confusion to a sense of rising panic. "Who are you? What's all this about?" His voice cracked and wavered.

"I promise, I will explain on the way, but we have to move now, please," John said.

"I'm not going anywhere. I have a presentation to give." Dr. Takada backed away from John, back toward the hall where he had been scheduled to talk.

John didn't want to say too much, but he couldn't afford to let the doctor get away from him now. "Doctor, I believe you've been targeted by a terrorist group. I think they plan on kidnapping you."

"That's preposterous! This doesn't make any sense. For all I know you're a kidnapper." Dr. Takada was beginning to put more distance between himself and John as he grew more concerned. "Just who are you anyway?"

"My name is John Stone. I'm here to help you. I have reason to believe that the Four Serpents want you. It's your kinetic weapons research. I think they are planning to use your work to launch another attack?"

The color drained from Takada's face. His eyes were saucers as the fear and confusion washed over his features.

"Why would they kidnap me for that? They wouldn't even have access to the type of equipment needed to manufacture or operate something like that," Takada said, almost to himself.

"With all due respect, doctor, underestimating the enemy, thinking they are low tech and living in caves, is a tremendous mistake. The moment you don't respect their full capability is the moment you don't come home," John said.

John reached a hand to grasp the doctor's arm gently, to guide him out of the building through a back exit. The doctor pulled away.

"Mr. Stone, let go of me. I have no desire to go anywhere with you. As far as I know, it is you that I should be afraid of." Dr. Takada spun on his heel and darted quickly for the door to get back to his presentation.

John let out an exasperated sigh. The doctor's suspicion of John only complicated the mission. He followed Takada back through the door trying to reason with him, but he was fully prepared to escalate the plan, and hoist the doctor up onto his shoulder, if needed.

The two stepped back into the conference preparation room, and John weighed the risks of taking the doctor against his will. How much security was here with them? How could he get out of the convention center with a possibly resisting doctor?

All of those questions faded from his mind when he spotted two men standing and looking over the area from the door at the far end. John made eye contact with one as they froze in their tracks, stared in shocked surprise.

The assassin from the hospital recognized John in the same instant. With no hesitation, the man reached into his jacket and pulled out a machine pistol, pointing it toward John and Dr. Takada.

CHAPTER
17

Kaliq squeezed the trigger of his weapon, spitting a steady stream of 9mm Makarov slugs at John, and chaos erupted. John wrapped an arm around the doctor and drove himself toward the side door, leading back to the main stage. The assassin stopped firing when John got close to the doctor, and he and the other man charged toward the American.

John barreled through the door, which gave way under his considerable size. He pulled Dr. Takada out onto the stage, planning to run across to find another door. Once he stepped past the curtains, John saw the people in the room panicked and ducking down, or running for the nearest exits. All except four men, also armed with the Skorpion machine pistols.

The men saw John appear on the stage with Dr. Takada and rushed forward. None of them fired, not wanting to risk hitting the doctor with their shots, instead choosing to close the distance. The stage would be wide open shooting gallery if John ran across.

He saw a big black hard container on wheels, the type used to carry lighting and sound equipment for events like this. John knocked large case over onto its wheels, ready to roll it out into the open across the stage.

"Stay close, Doc," John said.

He pulled Takada close and darted behind the case. It wasn't big enough cover John entirely, but any cover the case could provide would be better than nothing at this point.

The doctor let out a shrill shout in protest, not wanting to follow. John grabbed him around the waist with one arm and shoved the case out across the stage. The four men made their way closer, still not wanting to fire at John and Takada.

John had the case halfway across the stage, holding the still struggling doctor when the assassin made his way through the rear entrance with his partner. John angled the case to block an assault from both directions and pulled it while he backed his way across the stage. Two of the four men split away to flank John.

"We're going to have to make a break for that door, Doc," John said, nodding his head toward the exit behind them.

Takada squirmed to get out of John's grip, his eyes wide in fear. It was time to move.

"Now," John said.

He spun for the door, abandoning the cover. He guided the doctor firmly in front of him with his hand. Takada tripped and sprawled onto the stage.

Dammit John thought. He reached down to scoop the man up on the run, but Takada rolled to his back and scrambled away from John. He got to his feet and ran, with his hands up, toward the assassin who had just stepped out onto the stage in pursuit.

Time slowed as John watched the doctor run willingly to the terrorists. He stomach dropped when he saw the assassin wave the doctor behind him, toward the other man. Dr. Takada looked back at John, with a look of relief on his face.

The realization hit John far too late. Takada was working with the Four Serpents.

The assassin's partner escorted Takada off the stage, leaving five armed men against John. With the doctor out of their line of fire, all of their guns opened up. John rushed and dove off the stage, dropping out sight. He hit the floor hard on his side, fighting to keep the breath in his lungs.

John only had one option for escape, and his enemy also knew he was going for it. He had to escape fast before the five gunmen overran him. Their bullets continued in controlled bursts, chewing up the edge of the short stage and punching holes into the door through which he needed to escape.

On this side of the stage, all he had within reach were a few of the stackable chairs left behind the curtain. Maybe the curtain could be useful for concealment, if he could detach it from the high steel rigging posts around the stage. Could he bring down the steel rigging to cover his escape?

John crawled along the ground on his elbows, staying low until he reached one of the steel posts. He gave it a full force stomp with one boot. Steel supports shook and rang out from the impact, sending a violent tremor across the stage. The firing stopped for a moment when the assailants felt the floor move.

Despite his size and the force of his kick, the post did little more than vibrate and ring. He wouldn't be able to bring it down, much less damage it. The covering fire resumed, inching closer. John's only exit was directly in the line of fire.

"It's gut check time," John said to himself through clenched teeth.

Springing into action, he charged away from the stage, heading for the back of the room, instead of the door closest to him. The serpents adjusted their aim, moving to track him. *Perfect.*

They had done exactly what he hoped for. Before John cleared the curtain, he grabbed a handful of the thick black fabric and whipped it forward, to conceal his next move. Bullets tore through the heavy curtains. A hot flash of pain ripped across John's shoulder as one of the rounds bit into his flesh.

John used the distraction to double back. He grabbed the metal stacking chair, and hurled it at the assassin on the stage, aiming for his chest. The gunman whirled deftly out of the way, and John barreled out the exit door. Bullets ripped through the walls around him, and he dove to the ground once he was in the hallway.

John rolled until he was clear and stood up to escape.

The doctor. If I can cut off his escape, I might be able to grab him and get out, John thought. With what, though? He was outmanned, unarmed, and wounded. There may be more serpents waiting to help Takada get out. If that were the case, John would be running right into a firing squad.

He shouldered his way through another set of doors. Automatic weapons exploded to life behind him, and a few rounds whizzed past his head.

Two armed security personnel stepped into John's path, about 10 meters ahead of him.

"Five men with automatic weapons!" John yelled at the guards. "Get down!"

The guards would not be prepared to take on the terrorists, and he wanted to warn them before they stepped right into a meat grinder. One of the men took a knee, with his pistol aimed at the door, toward the sounds of gunfire, and the other used the corner for cover. Perhaps they didn't understand what John was saying in English. These two were either very brave or very foolish.

Two serpents came through the door first, weapons up. The guards fired, wounding one. He fell back through the door, as the other returned fire in the guards' direction. The two men did their best to hold their ground, but when the other men came through, they were overwhelmed by the sheer volume of fire.

A burst of automatic fire stitched through the kneeling guard's chest, and he sagged to the floor. Before he completely collapsed, John ran over and scooped him into one arm, pulling him back around the corner, behind the second guard. John grabbed the Beretta 92S from the wounded man's hand and a spare magazine from his belt.

John stood and leaned around the corner, over the other guard, and fired at the terrorists. They were spread out now, and unable to pursue John. Voices

133

approached from behind, and John turned to see more security guards coming, responding to the firefight. Three men arrived and looked at their man returning fire, then at the one that had been severely injured.

"I'll get him clear. You help your friend hold them back!" John yelled over the gunfire. He grasped the man by his collar and dragged him away from the fight. After pulling the injured guard down the hall, he reached a man directing the people out to safety. John knelt and applied pressure to the wounds on the man's chest as he called for a medic.

The man directing people ran over and crouched down to help however he could. The man looked around and said something quickly in French, before bolting through a door not too far away.

John kept his head on a swivel, looking for any other terrorists that might be around while keeping constant pressure on the man's wounds. The security guard's breathing was fast and shallow. John felt his heartbeat speeding up, a result of his blood loss.

John caught a glimpse of Dr. Takada moving through the crowds of people fleeing. The terrorist with him kept the weapon tucked into his suit jacket, out of sight, as they pretended to flee using the mass of people to cover their escape. John fought his instinct to race after them.

The man he was helping had little chance of surviving as it was, but leaving him on the floor would all but guarantee his fate. He bit down, tightening his jaw, and focused on every detail he could about the two fleeing men.

The firefight died down, leaving John to wonder if the security guards had stopped any of the terrorists, or if the serpents had overpowered them. He bristled as he prepared to face those men again. At that moment, the door near him opened and the man that left him seconds ago emerged with a large medical kit, yelling something into his radio.

The man slid to a stop near John and threw the case open. He put the radio down and ripped out some gauze pads from the trauma kit. Another man came running in from another direction, and John nearly stood to face a new threat. He stopped once he realized it was a paramedic, coming to help the wounded man. John was little help for the man, now that trained medics had arrived.

"I have to go," he said, knowing they didn't understand.

John stood and headed for the crowd where he last saw Takada and the terrorist fleeing.

* * *

The aroma of fresh coffee wafted out into the hall as the receptionist, Diana, brought a tray into the conference room. Gavreau and his teammates had been working since late last night, once they uncovered Brassard's betrayal and brought him in for questioning.

Gavreau sat at Lussier's desk, watching over his shoulder as he ran the names from the data drive through their database to cross-reference them.

"How are you doing, Alban?" Gavreau asked.

Lussier leaned back and stretched his arms high, arching his back to work out a kink. Then he exhaled long and said, "It's taking a bit of time, sir. Many of the names in Keppler's ledger are not on our database, but just being in the ledger is enough to warrant a deeper search. I haven't even gone through his notebook yet."

"Can we confirm Brassard's data in the ledger?" Gavreau asked.

Lussier paused. "I think so. We would need authorization to look into his financial records to be one hundred percent. But from what I see here, it is evident that Brassard has been receiving payments from someone that we can likely connect to the Four Serpents."

Gavreau looked away from Lussier and his computer monitor, as if not seeing the data would somehow make it not true.

How could you do this, Chris?

Deschanel burst into the room, heading straight for Gavreau, "Sir, there are reports of shots fired at the Paris Convention Centere!"

Gavreau instinctively shot a glance at the interrogation room where Brassard sat handcuffed, wondering if this was somehow something they could have prevented if he had cooperated.

"Coordinate with the Police Nationale. Get the details, and tell them we're on the way," Gavreau said. He turned to the rest of the RAID team. "Gear up. Standard load out."

* * *

John caught sight of Dr. Takada and his escort breaking away from the crowd to head out a side door. He was too far behind to catch up, pushing through the crowds. He cut across the panicked convention goers, and made his way to the door, barreling through without breaking stride, and saw a short hallway running left to right. Both sections turned 90 degrees and out of his sight.

Which way did you go? John thought.

He picked the right side randomly, knowing even a wrong decision made quickly would be better than indecision, and he had no time to spare. John bounded around the corner and ran down a long service corridor, heading straight for the large double door marked "Exit" at the far end.

There were doors along the hallway, on both sides, but John had to assume they were looking to escape quickly. He sprinted down the hall ignoring the other rooms and rammed the exit door open with his shoulder.

John ran further into the underground parking structure. Parked cars had occupied many of the parking spots. John heard nothing. He cursed himself, thinking he was too late, ready to double back.

The throaty rumble of a car engine pulled him back. He started in that direction with no hesitation, as the roaring engine and squealing tires got closer.

A car whipped around a concrete pillar, and John found himself face to face with Dr. Takada. The doctor's eyes grew wide, but the man driving the car accelerated, playing a game of chicken.

John brought the Beretta up in a one-handed grip and fired into the windshield. The driver swerved at the sight of the pistol, and John's shots missed his head by inches. The car angled back toward him, but

John stood his ground and fired twice more before his slide locked open on an empty chamber.

The driver lost control for a moment, the car shuddered and swerved. John saw, through the spiderweb crack on the windshield, that he had scored a hit. The driver pressed one hand to the side of his neck. He hoped that would be enough to force the car to stop, as he prepared to run over to the vehicle and retrieve the doctor. He had no such luck. The driver accelerated again and angled right toward him.

John leaped from the path of the car, nearly getting clipped as it passed. He rolled painfully into his wounded shoulder and came up into a crouch to see the car speed away. John grunted and ran toward the car, not wanting it to get away. He ejected the empty magazine from the Beretta and reloaded it on the run.

When he exited the parking area, he watched the sedan swerving around vehicles in a traffic jam, resulting from the chaos of the shooting in the convention center. John caught a break when the car slowed to a near stop, struggling to get clear of the jam.

He sprinted as fast as he could to close the distance, but they were just too far away for him to reach. He skidded to a stop, widened his stance and tried to slow his breathing.

His heart hammered in his chest, the rush of blood filling his ears and causing the sights of the pistol to pulse with each beat. John sighted the tires of the vehicle and waited until he had a clear shot that didn't put any civilians at risk. The car was nearly away when his window of opportunity finally came.

With even pressure, he squeezed the trigger three times with control and saw the sparks coming off the rim of the tire. His last shot scored, and he was rewarded with the front end of the car dropping as the tire went flat. Sparks showered from the escaping vehicle, and John put his head down and took off running for them again.

"Arrêt!"

John heard someone shouting behind him. More voices joined as police officers swarmed him.

He had been so laser-focused on the car, that he didn't register the French police around him, pointing their weapons. He stopped abruptly, the pistol held low at his side and watched the sedan screech away on the flat tire.

"They're getting away!" John said, pointing to the car with his empty hand. That movement set the police on edge, and they were moments away from opening fire on John. He had no choice, but to let the serpents escape with the doctor. John dropped the pistol to the ground, and raised his hands, lacing his fingers behind his head.

He narrowed his eyes, and his breaths came out in deep aggressive huffs as one of the police officers grabbed his wrist.

CHAPTER
18

"Three civilians were killed in the attack. Seven more wounded," the officer in charge relayed to Gavreau. "Including two security personnel and the American you asked about. John Stone."

The RAID commander and his team spent the last half hour securing the convention center. He thanked the officer and finished writing in his notebook, tucking it back into a pouch on his vest.

The American was in the custody of the French Police now. They had treated his injuries and made it a point to let Gavreau know he saved the life of a security guard injured in the firefight. Lionel wanted to have him transferred to RAID HQ and held there.

He was at his wit's end of watching this man operate with impunity on French soil. For all Gavreau knew, this shootout was a result of Stone's actions. When he was arrested, Stone was holding the pistol of the critically injured officer.

"Would you like to question him?" the Police Nationale officer asked.

"I'd like to throw him in a cell and lose the key," Gavreau said. He finally let out a sigh, ran a hand through his hair, and said, "Take me to him."

The officer led Gavreau to a police car parked at the perimeter of the scene. The American sat in the back, looking calmly straight ahead with his hands still cuffed behind his back. Gavreau wondered how they even got him into the back seat, as he seemed almost too large to squeeze through the door. The officer opened the back door and stepped away to handle other business.

Gavreau leaned on the door and stared at Stone for a long time before he finally spoke.

"I do not know what to do with you, Stone," was all he could think to say.

"Dr. Steven Takada is working with the Four Serpents," John said, as if they were in a briefing room, exchanging intelligence, and not locked up in a squad car.

"Enough. I told you we don't want your involvement. Look at what happened now? You are on the news, you know?" Gavreau said in his passable English.

John saw the news trucks filming him in the car, and he heard someone had captured his exploits firing at the fleeing car on a cell phone camera. He nodded to Gavreau and tried to continue.

"We have to find them, I know someone that can help—"

"We do not need your *help*," Gavreau cut him off.

He wanted to say more to the American, but he just pressed his lips together and closed the door, resisting the urge to slam it shut. John looked through the window at Gavreau with an intensity that some might have mistaken for anger. He saw determination, however, and he knew this would not be the last he saw of the American. Gavreau was at the end of his rope and walked away to cool off.

"I heard he saved that security officer," Deschanel said, walking beside Gavreau now.

Gavreau shook his head, no longer wanting to hear about the heroic actions of the meddling visitor.

"I don't know what to do with him," the RAID commander said.

"Look how far he got on his own. Maybe we could help him a bit, or just aim him at the bad guys and let him loose," Deschanel said.

Gavreau shot him a glare. Deschanel faltered for a step and put up his hands in surrender.

"Just a suggestion, sir," he said.

"When you're done giving me unhelpful advice, I want you to get in touch with central command. Have

144

them grant us access to the CCTV footage for a ten block radius. We also need satellite surveillance to find where the Four Serpents are taking Dr. Takada," Gavreau said.

"You think he's involved? Like, working with the enemy?" Deschanel asked.

"I don't know, but no matter whose side he's on, Takada is in the custody of the enemy now."

"Have you made a decision about him yet?" Deschanel asked, tilting his head over to John in the back of the police car.

Gavreau stopped and looked back at John. Then he shook his head and said, "Have him remanded into our custody. John Stone has the information we need to continue this investigation. I want to know everything he knows."

Deschanel nodded an affirmative and turned back.

CHAPTER
19

Bièvres, Essonne

Gavreau parked his car in his assigned spot at the RAID headquarters. Another vehicle parked nearby. Deschanel stepped out and opened the back door. John Stone's immense form emerged.

He was still in handcuffs, but Gavreau thought remaining in the restraints was optional for a man like Stone. The two men escorted John into the front entrance of the building.

"We are going to take you to interrogation, and you will assist us in our hunt for the Four Serpents," Gavreau said, his statement more of an order given to the American.

The ride in the elevator was tense, as the two RAID men were prepared for Stone to suddenly decide he no longer wanted to be in custody. The beep of the lift was a relief, and Deschanel did not entirely hide that in his face.

The trio stepped out of the elevator into a minor commotion in the common area. Gavreau saw a man he didn't recognize talking to the other RAID members around the desk. The man turned to face them when he heard their footsteps approaching. John straightened up a little, and Gavreau saw a small amused smile hiding under his mustache.

"Good afternoon gentlemen. Lieutenant Curtis Clarke," the man said, extending a hand to shake with Gavreau and Deschanel.

"What can we do for you, Lieutenant Clarke?" Gavreau asked, apprehensive about the answer.

"Sir, this man came here to—" one of the others in the room started, before Gavreau waved him off with a hand.

Clarke looked at the man that spoke, then back to Gavreau. The friendly but professional look never left his face.

"I'm here on behalf of the United States government. I have official orders to have John Stone remanded into my custody. I will escort him out of France and back home," Clarke said. "Out of your hair, if you will."

"What is this about?" Deschanel asked.

"Let's call it *diplomacy*. These two terrorist attacks occurring in the same week are a critical use of your resources. Lieutenant Stone," Clarke said, sure to use

John's previous military rank, "has been a thorn in your side during that time. All he wanted to do was to find the ones responsible for the death of a friend."

Clarke paused, a somber look on his face. Gavreau suspected Marvin Van Pierce was also a friend of Lieutenant Clarke.

"In the interest of preventing an international incident, and in light of his distinguished service record, I am here to escort John Stone back to the states," Clarke said.

"On whose authority?" Gavreau asked.

"The U.S. State Department," Silvestre said, holding some freshly printed pages in his hand.

"I was letting the rest of your team know, as you arrived. I assure you the request is official, and it has the approval of your government," Clarke said.

Gavreau snatched the papers from Silvestre and looked them over. He frowned and shook his head slightly.

"This man is directly involved in our search for the terrorists. His actions may have aided in their evading capture," Gavreau said.

John bristled, but stayed quiet.

"How are we supposed to just let him go? What if he might have information critical to our investigation?" Gavreau asked.

Curtis put on his best reassuring smile. "He doesn't have to go right away. You can ask him whatever questions you need to ask. I'm sure he will cooperate fully. After that, all I ask is that you allow us to leave here and head straight for the airport," Clarke said.

"We really have no choice, sir. The documents are official, signed by members of both nations," Silvestre said.

"Fine, take him to interrogation, and debrief him. I want to know everything he knows about the Four Serpents. Everything," Gavreau said.

Curtis nodded and followed one of the RAID men with a hand on John's back guiding him along.

Gavreau waited until they were out of earshot before talking any further.

"Did you get anything more from Brassard?" he asked.

"I'm afraid not," Silvestre said, shaking his head. "He clammed right up. He won't be a reliable source of information anymore. We moved him to a holding cell now."

Gavreau nodded and looked off into space, thinking.

"What are we going to do with him?" Silvestre asked.

"I don't know," Gavreau answered honestly. This man was part of their family, but his betrayal cut to the bone. Could they live with the decision to lock him up and throw away the key?

* * *

In the harsh lights of the interrogation room, John sat at a table, no longer wearing the handcuffs.

"Thank you very much for answering our questions, Lieutenant Stone. Your information will be of great help to our investigation," Cartier said.

They all stood to leave, and John allowed the interrogator to exit first, before whispering to Clarke.

"I have no intention of leaving, Curtis," he whispered.

"Believe me, Stone, I know," Curtis replied under his breath.

Months ago, when John was accused of committing acts of domestic terrorism on U.S. Soil, a charge that was eventually proven false, Curtis Clarke had been tasked to bring Stone to justice.

Clarke had butted heads with the man then and knew full well how Stone would be, when determined to achieve his objective. They walked back to Gavreau's office. Clarke knocked on the door and stuck his head in through the opening.

150

"Everything is all wrapped up here. Thank you for your cooperation in this sensitive matter," Clarke said.

"One of my men will accompany you to the airport," Gavreau said abruptly.

"No need, sir. We can find our own way. You've got your hands full," Clarke said.

Gavreau gave him a suspicious look.

"You need a ride there. One of my men will take you," he repeated.

Clarke shook his head slightly, then shrugged. "Okay, thanks for the offer," he said.

Gavreau picked up the phone and made a call to one of his men, to escort John and Curtis out of the headquarters. He was very clear about driving them directly to the airport, looking at Curtis and John as he spoke.

CHAPTER
20

Dr. Steven Takada fixed his gaze on the concrete bunker, as they approached in a nondescript sedan. Takada and the driver switched vehicles twice and took detours that led them through tunnels and other areas that restricted the view of any surveillance. They were here to meet with Azhaar bin Hashim, the leader of the Four Serpents, and had to minimize the chances of someone finding the base.

The *Serpent's Lair* was an impressively large warehouse area, located on the outskirts of town. The Serpents conducted all of their sensitive research and experiments indoors, in the reinforced, high ceiling hangar bays. Armed guards patrolled the area, waving the car through as they passed.

"What's in there?" Takada asked.

"You'll see that soon enough, Doctor," the driver said.

Kaliq approached the car as they pulled up to the main building, parking near a collection of random cars and trucks. He opened the door and helped Dr. Takada out, taking him to bin Hashim.

Takada retreated a step when the assassin greeted them, uncomfortable around the unpredictable man. Kaliq rarely spoke and showed little emotion when he did.

He led Takada up a set of metal stairs against one of the inside walls of the hangar. It led them to a set of offices high up, with large windows affording a view to anyone in the office to see what was happening in the hangar bay. They entered through the heavy door, which opened up into a large reception area. A hallway led to the entrances to the two adjoining offices.

Inside the reception room, a bearded man was speaking to another man in a language Takada didn't understand.

"Yes, sir. It will be done," the man responded in English, then he left the room. The other man turned to face the doctor.

"Dr. Steven Takada. It is a pleasure to finally meet you. I am Azhaar bin Hashim, and you are going to help us wake the world." Bin Hashim spoke English with only the slightest Arabic accent. He extended a hand to the doctor, who shook it with some trepidation.

"What happened at the convention center? Who was that man?" Takada asked. He was visibly shaken.

"Don't worry about him, dear doctor. He is simply a pebble in my shoe. That man is in the custody of the police so we won't have to worry, for now," bin Hashim said.

Takada pressed his lips tighter and nodded, still not convinced. "They know I'm helping you," he said.

Bin Hashim raised an eyebrow, amused at the comment. "Yes, good doctor. *They* know you have pledged your loyalty to the Four Serpents and our greater cause. Soon the world will know." Bin Hashim leaned in and lowered his voice. "All who have not given the Four Serpents their full allegiance will fall before our might, right Doctor?"

Takada swallowed. "Yes. Of course." He gave a quick nod.

"Excellent! I assure you that there is nothing that stands in the way of our success in this great mission," bin Hashim said.

He put an arm around Takada's shoulder, guiding him to one of the adjoining offices. Bin Hashim opened the door and ushered him through, following close behind. Takada looked around at the modest office setup, with a new computer set up at the desk. The boxes and bags of parts were still stacked in a corner.

"This workstation is isolated from everyone. No network or internet connection, and no remote connectivity. You will set your work up here," bin Hashim said.

Dr. Takada nodded and looked over the computer, approving of the setup.

"My work. I left it at the convention center," Takada said.

Bin Hashim's face changed at hearing the news. His features sharpened as he stared through the doctor.

"What did you say?" bin Hashim asked.

"My work. Everything happened so fast with that big guy trying to take me, and your guys shooting at us, I left my work at the table, where I was setting up for the presentation."

Bin Hashim's face went deep red, and he was on the edge of losing his temper. Before he could blow up, Dr. Takada tried to calm him.

"It's not a big deal. I have all of my data saved on a cloud network. I just need to access it to download everything, and I'll be back on track," Takada said.

"But you see, it is a *big deal*," bin Hashim said through clenched teeth. "All of your research, the research that you are here to complete, is now in the hands of the Police Nationale and RAID,"

"Yes, but I won't need that once I have my backups downloaded," Dr. Takada said, oblivious to the fact that his research in French government hands would mean they now know what the Four Serpents could be working on.

He also didn't fully grasp that bin Hashim wanted all of the computers in this area to stay offline, for security purposes. Downloading Takada's data online would expose this base to unnecessary risk. The doctor was ever so naive which could prove to be a significant detriment to the mission.

Bin Hashim considered, for just a second, if he could just kill Takada and try to continue on without him. In the end, he decided he still needed the doctor. Tying off all loose ends later, however, was now a real option.

"Kaliq, please have one of our computers set up with an online connection, and bring Dr. Takada with you, so he can download everything he needs," bin Hashim said.

The assassin nodded and escorted Dr. Takada away. Azhaar bin Hashim took a moment to calm himself, then walked to the office window. He looked down at the panel trucks parked inside, with the rear doors opened. A forklift rumbled as it backed away, pulling out pallets loaded with what looked like parts to assemble a small plane.

The leader of the Four Serpents assured himself that they were far enough along now, that their enemy's knowledge of their plan would not stop the mission from succeeding.

* * *

At the Orly International Airport, the silver Peugeot pulled in to the passenger drop-off. John remained quiet, but Curtis Clarke chatted with the driver the entire way. By the time they arrived, the driver's relief was visible in his face.

The man put the car in park and Curtis said, "Oh are you coming with us, to make sure we find our flight okay?"

The man closed his eyes, and his head dropped for a moment. He just wanted the incessant talking to end.

"No, you go ahead. I am sure you will manage," the man said.

"Oh, okay. Well, thank you all so much for your cooperation in this sensitive matter," Curtis said to the man, who just nodded in return. The two Americans stepped out of the car and walked through the entrance. John heard the sound of the car speeding away.

"Thank God for that. I thought I would have to hear that *chatty Kathy* act all the way to the gate," John said.

"What act?" Curtis asked, amused.

"I will punch you through a plane if you keep talking," John said.

Curtis chuckled, then pulled out his phone. He typed a text message and walked deeper into the airport.

"I appreciate the help getting me out of that spot, but I have no intention of leaving here right now," John said.

He expected resistance and was surprised to hear the opposite.

"I knew you would say that. Where to?"

"We need to find where they took Takada," John said, looking at the signs around them. "Get Parker on the line, find out if there's anything he can do."

Curtis chuckled, dialing Parker's number.

"What's so funny?"

"Seems that our little hacker friend knew you would be asking for some assistance, so he—" Curtis held up a finger. "Hey, Parker. I got John with me. I'm putting you on speaker."

"Hey John. I've been digging around, and I think I may have found something," Parker said.

John raised an eyebrow. "What do you mean you've been digging around?"

"Didn't Curtis tell you?" A faint clicking filled in the gaps between Parker's words. *"I had him run some software on the RAID systems."*

"You did what? When were you going to fill me in, Curtis?"

"Now," Curtis said. "Before I flew out here, Parker sent me some files to copy onto this." He held up a small flash drive.

John turned to face Curtis. "Are you telling me you just opened up the French national police computers up to an American citizen? A civilian at that. Do you realize how hard this could land on us?"

"On me," Curtis said. "I'm the one that uploaded it."

"They won't be able to trace it back to either one of you," Parker said. *"It's pretty ingenious, actually. The way it works is—"*

"I don't need to know the details, Parker," John said. "Look, what's done is done. I'll clean up this mess once we find Dr. Takada. Did your little program conjure up an answer?"

"I mean, it's not that simple."

"Yes or no, Parker," Curtis said.

159

"I—Yes. Or at least I've got my fingers on the most promising thread from Gavreau's case files." Parker typed away at his keyboard for another moment. "John, that car you saw the doctor get into was spotted by several witnesses."

"Perfect. Send the location to Curtis. We'll grab a car and head there now," John said.

"Well, RAID is tracking the car now, but they don't have a location yet," Parker said.

John's mouth formed a straight line. "Alright, when you do get the location, send it over right away."

"And what do you mean *grab a car*?" Curtis asked.

CHAPTER

21

Bièvres, Essonne - RAID Headquarters

Gavreau stared down at the page of notes on his desk. *What have you done, Doctor..* He sat back and wiped his hands across his eyes. "Dammit, Brassard. How did I not see it?"

"Sir," Silvestre said, knocking on the already opened door of the office. "You wanted us to let you know when we found the vehicle that took the doctor."

"Yes, thank you. Did you find where they are taking Takada?"

"Not yet," Silvestre said. "The vehicle has been spotted on several CCTV cameras already. They've abandoned it, switching to a car of the same model."

"Great job. Keep me appraised of the situation. Have the rest of the team ready to move out."

Silvestre nodded. "Sir."

Gavreau stood. "Just a minute." He walked over to the door placing a hand on the agent's shoulder. "Brassard was one of us. I understand how that may affect the morale of the team, but we must stop bin Hashim before the Serpents strike again."

"Understood, sir." Silvestre nodded again, his face showing a level of resolve that let Gavreau know his words got through.

He watched the younger man join the others, diving back into the mission. Gavreau laced his fingers behind his neck and stretched. He tightened his jaw and relaxed, feeling the tension slowly abate. *The blood of the innocents is on your hands, Christopher.*

The tension grew in his neck and shoulders again.

* * *

John looked over the Mercedes G-Class jeep that Curtis parked at the curb. "Where did you get this thing?"

"Some pimp just gave it to me. Says he didn't need it anymore," Curtis said, massaging the knuckles on his hand.

"Are you serious?"

"Does it matter?"

"I suppose not," John said, sitting in the passenger seat. "We've got a lot more to deal with right now.

162

Besides, this thing should still be in pretty good shape by the time we're done with it."

"Less the gas we're using," Curtis said, starting the engine.

"You get the location from Parker?" John buckled the seatbelt, staring off into the nighttime traffic.

"Yeah, we're about half an hour away." Curtis pulled into the street, merging with the cars flowing down the street. "Do you have any idea of what to expect when we get there?"

John shook his head. "Nothing good. At least half a dozen men armed with Skorpion SMGs. If bin Hashim is there, we can expect a lot more."

"Wonderful. Wouldn't have it any other way." Curtis smirked at John.

"I already know the answer, but I need to ask, did you bring any weapons with you?"

"Like you said, you already know the answer. Sorry, Lieutenant, but we're going to have to procure weapons on site."

"I hate last minute shopping," John said.

"Seriously, John, the location that Parker passed on is directly from RAID's system. Gavreau and the others know what we know." Curtis shot him a quick glance. "They'll be knocking the door down too."

"For once, we've got the advantage operating with a small team," John said. "They'll have to plan out their approach. Discuss tactics and contingencies for what they may run into on site."

"Part of that is gearing up," Curtis said. "That's the step I would rather not skip."

"Can't be helped," John said.

Curtis smiled, keeping his eyes fixed on the road. "Looks like we'll be renewing our subscriptions to Guns & Ammo when we get there."

John groaned. "You've been hanging around Parker too long."

CHAPTER
22

Bièvres, Essonne - RAID Headquarters

"And this information is accurate? Up to the minute?" Gavreau pressed a finger onto the file sitting in front of him.

"Yes, sir," Deschanel said. "We've got a request in for satellite surveillance as well. But this information is ninety-eight percent accurate."

"Excellent. Have the men ready to roll in five. We'll discuss tactics en route." Gavreau stood and nodded to Deschanel, heading out to join the rest of the team.

* * *

Serpent's Lair

Hurried footsteps filled the temporary workspace. Azhaar bin Hashim looked around as his men carried out his commands, preparing the equipment to Dr.

Steven Takada's specifications. They had assembled the components necessary for him to launch the weapon, and now bin Hashim grew impatient as the doctor continued pecking away at his keyboard.

"What is the hold-up, Takada?" he asked, picking up a random piece of tech on the man's desk.

"Everything is on schedule. I'm just starting up all of the subroutines necessary before launch." Dr. Takada adjusted his glasses and looked up.

"You assured me that our first strike would require only minimal calculations," bin Hashim said.

"Yes, we won't need to account for many of the variables of a longer range target, but this initial salvo is still important to future attacks," Takada said, fingers still flying across the keys.

Azhaar clenched his fists and closed his eyes, the doctor oblivious to the man's frustration. He took a deep breath through his nose and exhaled audibly.

"Important How?"

Dr. Takada removed his glasses, cleaning them with a small cloth from his coat pocket. "I need to tie this all into the same targeting software, networked across various data servers for the drone to course correct, ensuring the best ballistic trajectory."

"Explain it to me without all of the technobabble, Doctor." Bin Hashim struggled to maintain his composure.

166

"Well, the targeting software pulls its data from various nodes to determine how local weather patterns will affect the javelin once it's in flight." He put his glasses on and pushed them up the bridge of his nose. "These are unguided projectiles, so accounting for wind speeds, temperature, and humidity will ensure the most precise strike."

"Why is that all necessary for this?" Azhaar gestured to the drone, modeled after America's MQ-9 Reaper. "Once it reaches the target airspace, it is only a simple matter of dropping the javelins on our enemies."

"It's not that simple—"

Azhaar bin Hashim slammed his fist onto the desk, rattling the monitor and keyboard. Dr. Takada's eyes widened as he drew his hands close to his chest, leaning away as fear flooded his features.

"You dare second guess me?" bin Hashim narrowed his eyes to slits.

"I—I, no. No, bin Hashim, er, sir. I—" Takada stammered as he readjusted his glasses.

Azhaar stared into the man's eyes, partially obscured by the thumbprint on one of the lenses. "Please explain to me why it *is not that simple*, Dr. Takada." He softened his tone but maintained the menacing edge in his gaze.

After several tense moments and deep breaths, Takada continued. "In order to maintain a high level of precision with the weapon, I need as much data as possible."

"Go on."

Takada nodded. "Right now, we have enough information to target a specific building, but with the right type of attack, I can gather even more. I will be able to tighten the formula and bring the effective radius to three meters. You will be able to target individuals with a high level of accuracy."

Azhaar straightened up and smiled.

Dr. Takada's confidence returned. "And I'm not talking about strikes at twenty or thirty thousand feet. A successful strike would allow us to target our enemy from great range, effectively *lobbing* the javelins at a great rate of speed from altitudes beyond the effective ceiling of most military aircraft."

"Thank you, Doctor," bin Hashim said. "That is what I wanted to hear. Now, how much more time do you require?"

"Uh, maybe an hour," Takada said. "We can get the drone up in half that time, and I can push the rest of the calculations through the network and upload it in flight."

"Very good." Azhaar turned, switching to Arabic. *"Kaliq, keep the doctor safe. Get him whatever he needs to complete his task."*

The assassin nodded, holding one of the tungsten-rich kinetic penetrator *javelins*, rocking side to side as he adjusted the angle of the projectile, letting its weight carry his body back and forth.

CHAPTER
23

The early evening air still clung to its warmth, and John pulled off his jacket, letting the breeze hit his skin. He and Curtis left the Mercedes behind and traveled the remaining few miles on foot, the exertion warming his body and joints, preparing him for the fight ahead.

Curtis rolled his sleeves up past his elbows and knelt in the shadows next to John. "I only see the one man," he said, pointing in the direction of a lone sentry, walking the perimeter.

"He's armed and alert," John said. "They may not be expecting company, but these guys definitely aren't taking any chances."

"It's open ground too," Curtis said, shaking his head. "We would have to cover a good twenty yards to reach him. That's plenty of time to dump a mag into our bodies."

"That's if we're stupid enough to rush him from the front," John said. "I'm going to move around to flank him. When you see me in position, get his attention."

"In position? How am I supposed to know that?" Curtis whispered.

"I trust you," John said, making his way down the small slope to circle around the guard.

He could hear Curtis' frustrated curses as he moved. John made his way to a short row of bushes and belly crawled toward a pair of trees, giving him the best angle to approach the sentry. He waited for the man to double back before making his move.

As the man turned his back, John stepped onto the grassy strip to muffle the sound of his boots. He closed half the distance, only a short sprint away as his heart thumped in his chest. Before John could second-guess his plan, he heard a faint whistling in the distance. A terrible bird call sounded from where he left Curtis.

The sentry stopped in his tracks, leaning forward as his hand fell to his belt, pulling a flashlight.

John leaned his body forward, driving ahead into a full rush. The guard's light clicked on, but John's approach pulled the man's attention away from the whistling. He spun and whipped the beam behind him.

John carried his momentum forward, grasping the barrel of the man's AK-47, and thrusting the weapon upward to smash into the sentry's face, knocking several teeth loose. He followed with a sledgehammer, as his fist cracked the jaw of his opponent, laying him out.

Curtis ran the last few yards as the man's body hit the asphalt. He held his hands up, ready to join the fight.

"What kind of bird was that supposed to be?" John asked.

"That was a North American Smartass, smartass," Curtis said. "It worked, didn't it?"

John smiled. He untangled the rifle's sling from the unconscious guard, handing the weapon to Curtis.

"Thanks," he said, kneeling and checking the weapon's chamber.

John handed him a spare magazine and pulled a pistol from the holster on the man's hip. He eased the slide of the Sig Sauer P226 back enough to check for brass in the chamber. Patting the man down, he found no other weapons or ammunition.

"Grab his radio," John said.

Curtis pulled the device from the man's inner pocket and yanked the earpiece free, tucking it into his own ear. He fiddled with the dial before giving a thumbs up.

With a grunt John leaned over to retrieve the flashlight that the sentry dropped, testing the beam against his palm. "Let's go."

"It's your show," Curtis said, clutching the rifle close to his body as they moved toward the serpent's lair.

* * *

John reached a car similar to the one he saw Dr. Takada get into at the convention center. He placed a hand on the hood and peered into the distance.

"Still warm?" Curtis asked as he propped his rifle on the trunk, taking aim at the only building in the area.

"Barely," John said. "This is the same make and model. They must have switched cars on the way."

"How can you be sure?" Curtis asked.

John tapped the windshield. "No bullet holes. And the tire is intact."

Curtis smirked. "No, I mean, how do you know they're here?"

"I don't. Cover me while I head to that side door," John said.

"Wait," Curtis said, pressing a finger into the earpiece of the stolen radio.

"What are they saying?" John asked.

173

"They're speaking Arabic," Curtis replied. "I don't know what he just said, but my guess is that they're asking why our friend back there hasn't checked in. Should we wait and see what happens next?"

"No. We should move forward," John said.

As if on cue, the front and side doors opened as several men exited the building, carrying flashlights and spreading out. Each man held a Scorpion SMG in their other hand, slung close to their bodies as they began their search.

"Wonderful," Curtis said. "Looks like our friends have moved up the timetable."

"We can't engage them this far out," John said. "They would pin us down before we could get inside and find the doctor."

"Hide under the car?" Curtis asked, tilting his head to look underneath the vehicle.

John glanced down at the available clearance and held in a chuckle. "I think they would spot us like a rock under a doormat if we crawled under this thing."

He grasped a handle and held his breath as he eased the driver side door open. He sighed in relief when the car's cabin lights didn't turn on. John climbed in as Curtis did the same, laying across the back seats. Crawling over to the passenger side, John slouched down as much as he could, dipping his head below the dashboard, clutching the P226 in both hands.

Beams of light waved around, one passing through the windows of the car as the men spoke in hushed tones. One of the sentries passed along the rear of the vehicle, making his way to the outer perimeter, calling other men on the radio. Curtis listened in on the transmissions, still unable to make out the bulk of the discussion. The voices and light receded into the distance.

"We're clear, but it won't be long until they find our buddy snoozing in the shadows out there," Curtis said.

John opened the passenger door and slid out. "We'll deal with them later. I just need to get inside and see what we're up against."

"Later is about to be a lot sooner than we would like, John. We've got a rifle and pistol between us, and we just watched a half dozen men armed with fully automatic sub guns walk by us, in a perfect position to hit our flank when the shooting starts." Curtis checked the chamber of his weapon out of nervous habit as their situation grew more complicated.

John gave him a reassuring look. "Let's get inside. They may find the sleeper out there, but they won't know we've already infiltrated. By the time those guys get back, we'll be facing them head on."

"I'll never understand your mindset, Stone. Outmanned, outgunned, and you still think this is just some tactical hiccup."

By the time he finished his statement, Curtis had fallen in behind John as the two men covered the remaining distance to the side entrance of the massive facility. It was tall, with a curved roof and two rows of windows. Light from inside revealed a high ceiling, almost like a warehouse, or a flight hangar.

With no apparent runway, John couldn't make heads or tails of this seemingly out of place structure. He signaled for Curtis to stack up as he slowly turned the knob. Opening the door just a slit, John peered inside, taking in the scene once slice at a time. He wedged a toe into the gap and pressed his hands together on the pistol.

"Looks like eight, maybe ten men inside," John said over his shoulder.

"Great, just make sure you let me know before you go all *Rambo* in there." Curtis flicked the AK safety off and pulled it close to his body, settling the stock in front of his shoulder.

John nodded and slid his foot outward opening the door wide enough to slip inside. Curtis followed, using his lead arm as a wedge, entering right behind. The latch caught softly, cushioned by the pressure from the colder air inside.

They made their way along the wall, using the small shadow until one of the overhead lights bit a large circle out of their only cover. John looked around for a suitable replacement. Curtis followed his gaze, taking in the ten men John mentioned earlier. Two more strode along the walkway along the second floor, circling all the way around the structure.

Curtis nodded his head up to the men on the level above. "Those two are going to be a problem."

John didn't reply, fixing his gaze further into the building. "There," he said. "That's the guy that helped Takada escape the convention center. The assassin from the hospital."

In the distance, Curtis spotted a man in dark pants and a dark windbreaker. The man moved with short, shuffling steps, staring down at something in his hands occasionally.

"Are you sure?" he asked.

"I can see it in his eyes," John said, breaking away and moving to a set of crates further along the wall.

"Wait," Curtis hissed, balking before he followed.

John advanced again, getting closer to his target. The man grabbed a few more things off of a nearby table and walked up the stairs, heading into one of the offices on the next floor. Inside John could see Dr. Takada seated at a computer terminal.

There you are, Doc. John's grip tightened on the pistol. He clenched his teeth and sucked in a deep breath through his nose, ready to make his move.

"Hey!"

Shouting from behind him snapped John's attention back where he and Curtis were moments earlier.

"Intruder," one of the men on the upper level shouted.

Gunfire erupted, and Curtis brought the AK up to his shoulder, crouching behind one of the crates nearby. A jagged bloom of dragon's fire burst forth from the muzzle of his rifle as he returned fire.

John placed a pair of rounds from his P226 into the chest of a serpent grabbing a Skorpion from the bed of a truck. He turned back to the office above just as the assassin pulled the doctor out, heading down the stairs.

Takada struggled to keep up, holding the still opened laptop pressed to his chest. "Kaliq, please, you're hurting my arm."

John stood and took a step forward to pursue, but bullets sparked off of the metal support nearby, forcing him back behind cover. He propped his arms on the crate and returned fire.

178

CHAPTER
24

The smooth skin along the fuselage of the drone felt cool to Azhaar bin Hashim's fingers. The unmanned aircraft borrowed heavily from the American's MQ-9 Reaper. This would be the platform the Four Serpents would use to deliver a message to the free world.

He would remind the so-called *superpower* nations that even they can bleed. Dr. Takada's research would level the playing field, granting the Serpents the ability to target critical structures and people, instead of relying on indiscriminate bombings.

It was imperative that this initial flight succeed, not only in eliminating their targets but to gather all the data Takada needed to drastically improve their strike capability. The terror felt by the Western world would increase ten-fold with the Serpent's ability to launch a precision strike, without advance warning.

Azhaar bin Hashim closed his eyes and lifted his head, smiling as his victory was all but inevitable. Before he could bask fully, several loud cracks startled him. A string of automatic gunfire answered back. A firefight erupted in the front half of the facility.

"What's happening?" he shouted to one of his men. He grabbed the AK-47 leaning against a cart loaded with spare drone parts.

His bodyguard held a finger to his ear while shouting into his radio. After a moment he looked up. "We're under attack."

"That much I know, idiot! Go. We must keep the French police from getting their hands on the doctor."

The two men with him nodded and worked the charging handles of their rifles, before rushing toward the sounds of battle. Following close behind, bin Hashim looped the rifle's sling over his head and shoulder.

The large hangar portion of the back had two doors, each leading down a hall toward the office area in front. Bin Hashim stayed close to his men as two men rushed toward them.

"Hold your fire," bin Hashim said. "That's Doctor Takada."

"Thank you," Takada said, rushing to make his way past the armed men.

"Kaliq, what's going on?" bin Hashim asked.

His enforcer looked back and clutched his weapon closer to his body. Azhaar looked down the hall and caught a glimpse of a large, muscular man wearing dark pants and a black t-shirt.

"Is that the American? The one from the Paris Convention Centre?"

Kaliq snapped out of his stupor and looked bin Hashim in the eye. "Yes. American."

The sudden intensity of the man unnerved bin Hashim. He could see an odd fire in Kaliq's eyes. He couldn't figure out if he saw anger or determination. Either way, it could be harnessed.

He put a hand on Kaliq's shoulder. "You must stop the American. Do you understand? Do not let him pass."

Kaliq nodded and turned to face the enemy.

"What are we going to do," Dr. Takada asked, his voice shaky. "I need to get out of here."

The Serpent's leader struck the frightened man with the back of his hand. "You will accomplish your objective, Doctor. Upload the target parameters and get that drone in the air!"

* * *

John pressed the trigger five times in rapid succession, drilling a machete-wielding attacker. The slide of his P226 locked back, showing the empty chamber. John dropped the pistol and grabbed the machete, rushing ahead as a blur of movement whipped into his view.

John swiped his knife upward, knocking the terrorist's rifle off target. The machete's steel spine was still ringing from the impact when John plunged the wicked blade into the man's gut. The force of the blow carried the terrorist off his feet.

John ripped the AK-47 away with his free hand and fired a burst at another threat. In the distance, he spotted Takada turning to follow the other man down a hall.

Bullets chipped away at the walls and floor around both Americans.

"Curtis, watch my back. I'm going after the doctor!" John didn't wait for a reply before running behind a stack of opened crates.

* * *

Curtis popped his head up and fired a burst, scoring a hit on the second man above, sending him falling over the railing. He scooped a magazine off the floor, dropped by one of the terrorists he gunned down protecting John.

"Damn it, John," he cursed almost under his breath, shoving the spare into his coat pocket.

There was a brief respite in the firing as John disappeared into the hall. He could hear the serpents shouting at each other, organizing their actions. Curtis didn't give them a chance to capitalize and came up firing again, before running to a better position to watch John's back.

Bullets sparked off of the railing as he sprayed anywhere he saw movement, spoiling their aim. The AK clicked. *Empty.* Without hesitation Curtis pulled the spare magazine and used to strip the empty one free, rocking the fresh ammo into place and yanking the charging handle.

Before he could resume his assault, a sharp pain lanced across his outer thigh. He gritted his teeth and dropped back behind the crates John used as cover a moment earlier. Curtis looked down and saw the small tear in his pant leg. The blood wasn't bad, and the wound looked more like shrapnel, not a bullet.

Suck it up, soldier.

Curtis leaned out to one side, laying on the floor as several men made their move. Working the trigger with practiced ease, he let the rifle spit in pairs, sending six rounds down range. Each time one of the serpents would fall, although the last man did so more out of fear, retreating toward his friends.

A voice in his ear distracted him, shouting in Arabic. The men that left earlier to look for the missing sentry had just arrived. "Fantastic."

Curtis came up to a crouch and dropped the retreating man with a single shot between his shoulder blades.

CHAPTER

25

Two men stepped out of the hall to meet John. He fired the AK from his hip and gave the lead man an extended burst. Several of the heavy 7.62 mm rounds passed through and struck the second man, but it wasn't enough to drop him.

The serpent returned fire as he fell. John dove to one side, rolling on the hard concrete. He came up to a kneeling position and fired a short burst into the man's torso before elevating his aim enough to place a single shot in his forehead.

John grunted and ran toward the hall. As he rounded the corner, bin Hashim's formidable assassin blocked his path. With the speed of a serpent's strike, Kaliq snapped a hand out and lifted the muzzle of John's rifle.

A Glock 19 flashed up toward John's chest. John released his grip on the AK-47 with one hand and reached out. His fingers clamped over the thumb and wrist holding the pistol.

The Glock barked, and the slide bit into John's hand. Kaliq torqued his wrist to wrench the handgun free. The assassin circled it back and tucked it near his body in one smooth motion. John leaned into the rifle and swung the barrel in a full circle, looping toward his opponent's legs.

The Serpent's enforcer executed an unorthodox spinning flip to dodge the sweeping barrel. John had a difficult time tracking, much less anticipating, the smaller man's movements.

His AK chattered loud in the close quarters, bullets cracking the floor. Kaliq twirled back with a dancer's grace, firing his pistol as he evaded the incoming assault. The powerful concussive blasts thumped in John's ears. Immense muzzle flashes obscured his vision in the dimly lit hallway. He couldn't see his target clearly at that moment, but that meant his foe's visibility was also compromised.

Through the bright flares in the middle of his vision, he spotted Kaliq moving in. His AK met resistance, as the assassin pinned it against the wall with his foot. John snapped his hand out again, catching Kaliq's wrist before he could fire the Glock.

Both men locked eyes, and the moment in time stretched. John stared into an abyss, unable to read anything from the man's gaze. Kaliq was looking through John. A thousand yard stare.

With his opponent standing on only one leg, John thrust his head forward to drive him off balance. Kaliq leaned back and flipped away. He kicked John's wrist as he arced backward, knocking the rifle free. John felt the pistol fall from Kaliq's grip as well.

Seizing the moment, John stepped in and fired a jab. Kaliq tried to slip the blow, but John scored a glancing hit. He followed with a straight right, but the assassin deflected the punch and slammed a hard hook into John's ribs.

A foot snapped up, and John brought his arm up in time to absorb the roundhouse kick. He thrust out with a front kick to push the enforcer back. Kaliq twisted out of the way, continuing his rotation to send an elbow crashing across John's jaw.

The strike jarred his vision, filling it with stars. A kick pounded his thigh, and a second buried itself into John's gut.

Before his opponent could pull his foot back, John wrapped an arm around the ankle and brought his forearm down on the meaty upper leg. Kaliq let out a grunt and jerked his limb free, limping back before settling into a strange arrhythmic movement pattern.

Kaliq shuffled to his left, switching angles before reengaging. John pushed off his rear leg and twisted his body, launching his fist straight through his oncoming opponent. Kaliq's knee buried itself into John's solar plexus, driving the air from his lungs.

John dropped to his knees, a line of drool splashing on the ground. Even through the pain, John had felt his fist connect.

He couldn't match the smaller man's speed, so he took the full force of the incoming attack to land a punishing assault of his own. He clenched his teeth and pulled a breath of air in, ignoring the immense pain.

Kaliq leaned against the wall clutching his chest. The assassin spat on the floor and bridged the gap again. A palm strike collided with John's jaw, but he shrugged it off and buried a wrecking ball into Kaliq's gut.

The Ranger followed with a left hook, violently twisting the assassin's body away. Kaliq stunned John when he used the momentum to whip a spinning roundhouse kick at his head.

John managed to catch the man's ankle, his hand swallowing much of the joint. He grabbed a handful of Kaliq's jacket and swung him bodily into the wall, the impact shaking the doors.

An animalistic growl pushed past John's gritted teeth. He jack-hammered a right cross into the assassin's face. The powerful punch snapped Kaliq's head back through the wall with a sickening crunch. The force of the blow fractured his skull and snapped the assassin's neck, leaving him embedded in the wall.

John scooped up Kaliq's Glock 19 and ran toward the far end, in pursuit of Dr. Takada.

* * *

Dropping his AK-47, Curtis dove and slid across the polished concrete, snagging a Skorpion. He rolled behind a truck as the enemy's bullets cracked the ground nearby, peppering him with bits of debris. Flat on his stomach, he aimed the machine pistol at the feet of a serpent rushing his position. His rounds slammed into the man's shins and knees. The terrorist fell forward, cracking his face on the ground, sending a tooth skittering toward Curtis.

He frantically ejected the spent magazine and looked around for another. Maybe his luck would hold out, and the enemy wouldn't realize his weapon had run dry. He whipped his head to the side as a dull, metallic clanging rang out, the round object bouncing and rolling to a stop nearby.

Grenade!

His heart raced. Curtis scrambled to his hands and knees, grabbing the explosive and tossing it over the truck. Exploding in mid-air, the grenade shattered

190

all of the nearby windows. A shower of broken glass cascaded over his back as he held his hands over his head, bracing for the impact.

His ears rang, and he could feel his pulse in his eyeballs. *That was not fun,* he thought. By the time the buzzing whine in his head receded, he could hear the serpents shouting at each other. Apparently, one of them got a little too plucky and tossed a grenade, and the others didn't seem to approve.

Footsteps crunched on the bits of glass as an assailant moved around the truck. Curtis leaped up to his feet and shoved the serpent's rifle into the man's chest, forcing him on his heels. When the man pushed back, Curtis let him come forward and used his momentum to get behind his opponent.

He pulled the rifle up against his foe's neck, using him as a barrier, as they sidestepped to another stack of equipment.

Before he could reach cover, the terrorists opened fire, punching holes in his human shield. Curtis felt the body fall from his grasp. He dove to the side, still clutching the dead man's AK. Fire lanced up from his calf as he rolled the final few feet behind the crates.

Pressing a hand to the wound, his fingers came away bloodied. "Why do I let John pull me into these messes?"

191

More men shouted. Curtis rose from behind cover and triggered a burst to push them back. He shifted the sights to the side, scanning for an active threat. Stacked next to a forklift, Curtis spotted the tungsten rods. His finger tightened, and in that moment of hesitation, enemy fire drove him down.

Of course it's not something explosive that I could have used as a distraction. He crawled back behind another stack of equipment.

A volley of fire missed him by inches. More serpents had opened up from the front of the building.

He rolled to his back, firing behind him where the guards from outside had returned, flanking his position. Curtis sprayed a long burst in their direction and scrambled to his feet, making a break for the forklift.

Bullets chewed the crates and equipment as he passed by. He gritted his teeth to drive through the pain in his leg. Curtis dropped to a slide the last few feet. Sparks bloomed off of the forklift, just over his head. Two of the guards broke away and ran toward him, their Skorpions blazing.

Curtis grabbed one of the kinetic javelins and jammed it into the forward control of the forklift. The massive machine lurched and plowed ahead. Curtis took aim and shot down one of the guards that tried to avoid the forklift barreling toward him.

More serpents joined the fight, now. Curtis leveled his sights on a crowd and pressed the trigger. The rifle bucked several times before the bolt locked back. He cursed and pulled the spent magazine, looking for another weapon.

"Sorry I couldn't do more, John," he said.

His grip tightened on the steel mag. Curtis dropped the rifle and stood, hurling the magazine at the incoming soldiers. For a split second the lead man flinched, thinking it was a grenade. Just as the steel box clanked against the concrete, the air around them pulsed out as explosions rocked the room.

The serpents looked back in shock and Curtis glanced down at his hands. Ears still ringing, he could barely hear the additional combatants. French voices joined the chaos of the serpents' shouts. RAID had just stormed in, using breaching charges.

Gavreau and his team moved through the battle zone with trained precision, firing with disciplined control, dropping anyone that posed a threat, with no hesitation.

* * *

The pops and thumps of the firefight hardly registered this far back in the reinforced facility. John held his pistol, pressed between both hands, the front sight covering bin Hashim's upper chest in his view.

Azhaar bin Hashim, leader of the Four Serpents, held his AK-47 close to his body, muzzle pointed at John, while he used his other hand to swing Dr. Takada into the line of fire. Twenty meters of open hallway lay between them. John slowly closed the distance as he spoke.

"It's over, bin Hashim. If you don't think I'll put a bullet between the doctor's eyes to get to you, you're sorely mistaken." John's words echoed, adding to the sporadic crackling of the distant battle.

"My serpents will strike your friend down, and swarm in here to finish you off." Azhaar bin Hashim leaned out to one side. "And then the world will feel our wrath."

"P—please don't shoot me," Takada said, his voice cracking as tears streamed down his face.

"You had your chance to come with me," John said, advancing with slow, measured steps. "But it's not too late, Doc. Just run away. Let me and this dirtbag settle up."

"Enough!" bin Hashim shouted. "You've lost, and you know it, American. You'll never make it out of here alive."

194

"I don't need to make it out. I just need to stop you. Or perhaps I can just put Takada out of his misery. I'm guessing he hasn't given you what you need to accomplish your mission." John shifted his point of aim, just enough to cover the doctor. A smile spread across the Serpent leader's face.

"I have everything I need now," bin Hashim said.

He shoved Dr. Takada to the side and brought his rifle up. John aimed, and took the slack out of the trigger. Then, the entire building shook. Both men fired, their shots missing. Azhaar dove behind a pair of steel drums and John strode forward, shooting his Glock.

After the explosions from the battle out front, John heard the volume of fire escalate. There was no way Curtis would be able to hold back that number of men. He had to push ahead and get to bin Hashim fast.

The serpent lifted his rifle up over the barrel, spraying wildly. His blind volley of fire flew overhead, and John answered back. He fired the last round from his pistol and wasted no time to rush forward.

Azhaar stood and leveled his AK, but it was too late. John's shoulder impacted with the steel drum, driving it and the man behind it back toward the drone. With a swipe of his arm, John hurled the second drum out of the way, as he closed the distance.

Bin Hashim screamed and whipped his weapon up. John snatched the handguard and hoisted the serpent to his feet. He plowed a fist into bin Hashim's jaw, stripping the AK from his grasp. He let the rifle clatter to the floor and stood over Azhaar bin Hashim.

"Like I said. It's over." John's words echoed, no longer competing with gunfire.

The battle had ended.

"No," Dr. Takada said. "You can't kill him."

John glanced back over his shoulder as Dr. Steven Takada clutched the AK-47 awkwardly, tight to his hip, walking toward him.

John shook his head. "You're making a huge mistake, Takada."

"You hear that?" Takada said, circling around to help his leader. "Your friend is dead. The Four Serpents—"

John whipped his arm out, smacking Dr. Takada across the face with a backhand. The doctor spun, dropping the rifle, and collapsed to the floor, unconscious.

A flash of movement snapped John back. Bin Hashim drew a knife from his belt and lunged for the kill. John's hand swallowed the man's wrist. He squeezed, popping and separating the small bones.

196

Bin Hashim let out a shrill cry, dropping the knife. John snatched the blade in a reverse grip, as it fell.

"Hold this," he said as he plunged the blade into bin Hashim's thigh. The steel knife dug in deep, splintering bone as it split part of the man's femur.

Tears streamed down bin Hashim's face as he bellowed in agony. John spun him around and pulled him close, wrapping a tree trunk around the man's neck.

He secured a choke and leaned close, whispering into bin Hashim's ear. "I don't need to escape to win. I just need to rip the serpent's head from its body."

More men burst into the back, from where John had entered. He spun, using bin Hashim to shield himself from the assault.

"Let him go, Stone." A man wearing all black tactical gear stepped into the room, armed with an M4 carbine. He pulled the cloth away from the lower half of his face.

"Gavreau?" John kept his grip on the hostage.

"You cannot kill him," Gavreau said. "Let us take him in alive. He wants you to martyr him."

Azhaar bin Hashim gurgled, futilely pulling at John's massive arm with his uninjured hand. The American released his grip, letting the terrorist crumple to the floor, defeated.

"Where's Curtis?" John asked. "Is he alive?"

"Outside. My men are treating his injuries," Gavreau said.

Several RAID members moved up and secured bin Hashim in flex cuffs, while the medic wrapped bandages and gauze around the knife still buried in his leg.

Lionel Gavreau lowered his weapon and put a hand on John's shoulder. "It is over. We won."

CHAPTER

26

John pressed a finger to the bandage across the wound on his shoulder. He looked in the mirror, admiring the bruising on his face from his battle with bin Hashim's man, Kaliq.

"I see you got some work done," Curtis said, hobbling in on a set of crutches. He sat, using them to slow his descent.

"My modeling days have just begun," John said, pinching the bridge of his nose to make sure nothing had been broken.

Both men looked over as the RAID medical team wheeled Azhaar bin Hashim in on a gurney, heading for the elevator.

"I thought they'd take that guy to a hospital," Curtis said.

John chuckled. "There's no way they would risk that. My way would have simplified things."

"Gavreau was right. It's good that you listened to him." Curtis watched Dr. Takada stumble down the hall, hands cuffed behind his back.

"I know," John said with a solemn nod, taking a seat.

"Wow, that was much easier than I expected," Curtis said.

John's face softened as he looked down at his weathered hands, rubbing them together. "We got them, though. The men responsible for Van Pierce's death. But just like when we got Windham, it feels hollow. Like we've accomplished nothing."

Curtis pursed his lips. "Vengeance never fills the void. But the world is better off without the Four Serpents." He leaned back and pointed toward the sky. "For MVP."

"I'll drink to that." John pointed to Curtis' leg with the toe of his boot. "What happened, you get a muscle cramp? Did the medics give you a banana for the potassium?"

"Ha ha, tough guy." Curtis leaned to his left and looked at the bloodied bandage around the lower half of his leg. "That's a twelve pack you owe me. And not that supermarket swill you chug. I'm talking the good stuff."

Lionel Gavreau approached, holding his helmet tucked under his arm. "Gentlemen. I do not know what to say."

"I'm guessing *thank you* isn't one of your options," Curtis said gently probing the muscle around his gunshot wound.

"Not officially, no," Gavreau said. "But perhaps I can pass on some of the gratitude from a few of my men. Your reckless actions did make our jobs a little easier, I must admit."

"Our pleasure," John said with a crooked grin.

"We aim to please." Curtis pantomimed looking down the sights of a rifle.

"With the pleasantries out of the way, we all know that this entire investigation will require a lot of cleaning up between our governments." Gavreau's face hardened.

He handed his helmet and gloves to one of the other men and pulled a chair closer. "I cannot promise that any of us will escape without facing the repercussions of our actions."

"It should only be my head on the block," John said. "I'm the one that barged into your investigation. Neither one of you should have to face the consequences of my actions."

Gavreau chuckled. "It would almost be easier to explain that we helped you find your friend's killers.

The alternative would be to admit that we just let a foreigner step all over our case, obstructing us every step of the way."

"Well when you put it that way," Curtis started.

"Besides, you brought Brassard to our attention," Gavreau said.

"You were right behind me at Keppler's apartment. You would have found the data regardless," John said, standing up.

"But would I have allowed myself to see the truth?" Gavreau stood up and shook John's hand.

"If you don't mind, I'd like to stick around and hear what you get from Azhaar bin Hashim, and Doctor Takada," John said.

Gavreau looked at the bandage on John's arm and Curtis' crutches. "I believe you have earned that right."

* * *

Patrice Cartier exited the interrogation room, a satisfied smile crossing his face. Steven Takada held his head in his cuffed hands, on the table. Wracking sobs shook the doctor's body, torn apart by his guilt in joining the serpents.

Curtis watched the interrogator pass by with what looked like glee in his eye. "Does he always enjoy his job that much?"

Gavreau flipped his notebook closed and stood to exit the observation room. "Well when you have been trying to chisel the truth from a block of granite all week, it is nice to have an eggshell-like this crumble and spill everything."

John sat, still staring at the doctor through the double-sided glass. Curtis pushed himself onto his crutches to follow the RAID commander to the briefing room.

"You coming, John?" Curtis asked.

"I'm right behind you," John said, still boring holes into the interrogation room.

* * *

Silvestre and Deschanel passed John, giving him a quick nod as he entered the briefing room. Curtis had already taken a seat near the front, where Gavreau prepared bits of Dr. Takada's research data. The RAID commander flipped through the pages of his notebook, piecing everything together.

John took a seat next to Curtis, then Gavreau turned to point at the data on the screen, starting his *presentation*.

"The doctor's most recent research, as you know, focused on utilizing data from the global weather satellites to paint a more complete picture of shifting winds, temperature, and humidity to a high degree of precision," he said.

"I got that part," Curtis said, "but I thought his primary research was the kinetic-strike javelins. Was he using rain clouds to cover the attacks or something?"

"He's improving the accuracy of the weapons," John said.

Gavreau pointed in John's direction with his notebook, nodding. "Correct. The javelins are inert, tungsten-rich rods, with no guidance systems. They rely solely on the calculations handled up front, in order to hit their targets."

Curtis furrowed his brow. "What are we talking here, sniper-level accuracy? Fractional minute of angle from five miles up? These things hit hard, and don't require that level of precision to drop on an unsuspecting target."

The screen changed, showing a different set of calculations and diagrams.

"Agreed, that is a bit extreme," Gavreau said. "Takada's research wasn't about the effects of wind when deploying the weapons directly below. He was working on software that would grant the ability to *lob* the kinetic-strike projectiles over a great distance and still hit the target. The weapons would be silent and have no heat signature, making them all but invisible to our countermeasures."

"The answer to your first question is *yes*," John said. "Like a sniper taking shifting wind patterns and air temperature into account, Takada's software does the same on an international scale. Only instead of a mile or two, the drones would be making shots at hundreds, maybe even thousands of miles away."

"Thousands?" Curtis looked over at John.

"Theoretically," Gavreau said. "To accomplish that, the delivery system would have to operate far outside the parameters of the UAV we procured from bin Hashim's base."

Curtis leaned forward, resting his elbows on his legs. "Wow. And Takada transmitted his data right before we stopped bin Hashim?"

"Yes." Gavreau glanced down at his notebook. "His computer backed the research up to a cloud drive. We have since had the data remotely wiped."

John leaned back, folding his arms across his chest. "Shouldn't you have a team out hunting for anyone else that may have this information?"

"Yeah, we've got a guy that can help," Curtis said. "He just needs access to—"

Gavreau waved. "No. We cannot risk bringing too much attention to the search. We have bought time to track down and arrest any stragglers that might still be involved."

John tightened his jaw, looking at the RAID Commander.

Gavreau smiled. "My friends, this intel is also in your government's hands. Rest assured, our two nations will be working together to take care of the rest."

"What did we get from bin Hashim?" Curtis asked. "He should be able to fill in all of the gaps in the doctor's blubbering confessions."

"Nothing yet. He is still in surgery." Gavreau glanced over at John. "Apparently it is not a simple matter to safely remove a knife embedded in one's femur."

CHAPTER

27

"I'm gonna grab something to eat. I'll wait for you in the car," Curtis said, settling his weight on the crutches.

Several more members of the RAID unit walked over, smiling. They nodded at John and shook his hand.

"You are quite a celebrity," Gavreau said, stepping out of his office as he stuffed a stack of papers into a manilla envelope.

He handed the files and reports over to John.

"We had a rough start, but I wanted to say thank you," Gavreau said, shaking John's hand again.

"Curtis and I should be the ones thanking you for pulling our asses out of the fire back there."

"Yes, you should." Gavreau smiled. "Safe travels, my friend."

* * *

John started reading a text message from Parker when his phone buzzed.

"Parker, I was just reading your text."

*"Hey, John. Just wanted to make sure you saw it." * Parker's fingers tapped away on the keyboard as he spoke.

"You sent the message literally seconds ago," John said.

"So did you read it, yet?"

John sighed. "Just tell me what it says."

"Ok, but don't get mad at me," Parker said.

"What did you—"

"I read the reports from Doctor Takada's interrogation. No one seems concerned that his research is still out there," Parker said, his typing no longer filling in the pauses.

"Are you still connected to the RAID system?" John asked, lowering his voice as he turned toward a corner.

"Yes, but only to help them finish this case."

"Parker, you're unbelievable." John looked around before taking the stairs to the second floor. "You need to shut that program down now, and clean up all traces of your presence."

"I will, but I'm reimaging Takada's laptop to dig through it here," Parker said. *"I don't think Gavreau is concerned enough about this data falling into the wrong hands."*

208

John pinched the bridge of his nose, closing his eyes. "We've already captured bin Hashim. The Four Serpents are all but finished. Gavreau and his men will be putting a plan together to clean up the rest. They're already keeping tabs on other climatologists associated with the doctor, just in case."

After a long pause, Parker replied. *"Ok, but this the part where I need you to stay calm and not get mad."*

"We're a little past that already."

"I've downloaded all of the after-action body camera footage from RAID's team, just to make sure no key members of the Four Serpents escaped in the attack," Parker said.

"Are you nuts?" John hissed through gritted teeth as he turned to face the window at the end of the hall.

"I just need to be sure," Parker said. *"Doctor Takada's research isn't rocket science. It isn't going to take someone with a Ph.D. to figure it out at this point. Just some raw computing power, and access to global weather networks."*

John took a breath to gather his thoughts. "Parker, you have to cut the connection now."

"If those kinetic-strike javelins end up in another terrorist cell—"

"Parker! Now." John tightened his jaw as the phone creaked in his fist.

"Alright. I'm sorry, John," Parker said. *"Let me just end this query and—wait a minute."*

John listened as Parker started typing for what seemed an eternity. "What is it?"

Parker exhaled through his nose. *"I don't know. Could be nothing, but my mob recognition seems to think that there's something different about Azhaar bin Hashim."*

"Yeah, he's not going to be moving around the same as older footage, considering he had a six-inch blade jammed into his thigh," John said, still trying to contain growing frustration.

"Well, the facial recognition said it's the wrong guy, but facial recognition software is lame. I ran the mob program, and it's returning a seventy-two percent probability that it's him."

"Considering his condition by the time RAID arrived," John said, turning to lean his back against the glass, "it sounds like we've got the right guy."

"It's just that sub ninety percent probability means—"

Three shrieking thumps rattled the building in rapid succession. The interior walls and windows pulsed out, everything shattering. A concussive wave threw John out of the building. His breath was stolen from his lungs, and the fall lasted for minutes in his mind. An impact like a sledgehammer between his shoulder blades sent pain signals exploding out to his limbs. The back of his head slammed into the dented roof of the SUV underneath, and the impact of his landing blew out all of its windows.

John's vision swam through a tunnel of darkness that swallowed the world around him.

CHAPTER
28

John squeezed his eyes shut to drive out the blinding glare. Through his ringing ears, the muffled sounds of car alarms and sirens slowly faded as his head dropped back, unconsciousness dragging him under again.

CHAPTER

29

John tried to lift his arms, but his extremities were sluggish, moving through a taffy-like haze. Blood thrummed and rushed through his ears with every heartbeat.

Someone put a hand on his chest, shaking his body. A warbling buzz in his head slowly reformed into coherent words.

"John!" Curtis shook him again, "John, you gotta get up."

Curtis tossed his crutches to the side and helped him sit up. John groaned as he swung his feet over the fender of the SUV, sliding down to the asphalt. His boots crunched on broken glass, and he wobbled to keep his balance.

"What happened?" Curtis bent to pick up his crutches again.

"I don't know," John said, his voice hoarse. "I was on the phone with Parker when I heard something hit the building before it all exploded," John said.

He wiped a hand across his face and eyes, brushing the blood and dust away. His vision slowly pulled itself back into clarity, and John looked at what was left of the RAID headquarters. The entire northwest corner had collapsed, exposing the floors, wires, and plumbing. A sharp pain nearly dropped him to his knees as he sucked in a deep breath. The pop reverberated through his body, as a rib settled back into place.

Sirens wailed as first responders pulled up to the scene, racing from their vehicles to attend to the wounded. John waved a medic away, moving off to the side. He struggled to tell them they needed to help the other survivors, not understanding their replies in French.

"John, you need to let them check you out." Curtis handed him a bottle of water.

John swished a mouthful, spitting the bloody, dirty water out before draining the rest of the bottle. "Did anyone else make it out yet?"

The solemn look in Curtis' eyes told him plenty.

John pushed ahead, but Curtis and two of the medical techs tried to hold him back.

"We need to help Gavreau and his team! Let me go!" John shrugged the hands off and ran toward the building as another large chunk of concrete fell free, smashing apart in front of him.

He staggered back a step, covered his mouth with his arm and ran through the cloud of smoke, inside the wreckage of the RAID HQ.

* * *

Helping the first responders, John and Curtis spent the next hour pulling people out of the building. News crews swarmed, as the crowd outside grew. John lifted a woman out of the rubble, setting her on a nearby gurney when someone called out from inside, emerging from the stairwell.

"I need some help here," Gavreau said, speaking French as he carried a man his shoulders. *"He's lost a lot of blood."*

Silvestre pulled a chunk of concrete to the side and disappeared back into the stairwell before emerging with a woman leaning on him with an arm draped around his neck. Her face was bloodied, and her right leg looked mangled.

Another two hours passed. Then, police and medical responders no longer let John or the others back toward the building. A woman kept shouting at him in French as John tried to push past. She grew angry and shoved him hard in the chest, speaking sternly and waving for him to go back.

"She is saying it is not good for us to breath the air," Gavreau said. "Too much smoke and dust. Please, John, let them take a look at you."

John's shoulders sagged as the words sank in. He looked up to see the large crews working quickly to pull survivors out of the building, helping those they could, and evacuating the ones in more serious condition.

With a nod, he relented and turned back, heading to the ambulances.

"At least a dozen were inside the section that collapsed," Curtis said. "Several survived, but suffered serious injuries. Five more were evacuated, in critical condition."

"How many dead?" John asked.

"They still do not know," Silvestre answered. He tilted his chin as one of the paramedics finished stitching the cut over his eye.

"What about the rest of your team?" John asked Gavreau.

"Deschanel is dead." His words were almost inaudible.

Silvestre looked over, a mix of fire and pain in his eyes.

Gavreau looked up at John. "Lussier was evacuated half an hour ago. He may lose his arm." He swallowed.

"What happened?" Curtis asked.

"Kinetic-strike javelins," John said. "The Serpents are still active."

"I don't understand," Curtis said. "We captured bin Hashim. We've got his drone and the tungsten rods."

"Where is bin Hashim?" John asked. "Doctor Takada?"

"Dead," Silvestre said, spitting. "Both of them were in the northwest corner. I watched them pull out what was left of that terrorist filth."

"That rules out an attempted prison break," John said.

"Do you think they were trying to silence him. I mean the doctor already spilled his guts," Curtis said, looking at the ruins. "Figuratively and literally."

"I have to make a call," Gavreau said.

The RAID commander pulled a phone from his pocket and scrolled through his contacts as he walked away. Silvestre nodded to John and Curtis before going his own way.

"I should call Parker," John said, patting his pockets.

Curtis handed his phone over. "Yours didn't survive the fall," he said. "You were still holding it when you totaled the rental parked outside."

John pulled up the recent calls and selected Parker's number.

"Curtis, what's happening?" Parker asked. *"The news is saying there was an explosion in France."*

"It's John. I had to borrow this phone because mine was damaged in the attack."

"Attack? Are you alright?"

"Parker, we need to figure out what happened," John said. "I think the Four Serpents were able to piece the doctor's research together and hit us with the javelins."

Parker's fingers clicked across his keyboard in the background. *"That's a likely scenario, but it just feels too fast to organize that type of plan."*

"We need to know what we are up against. Is there anything you can do to figure out what might have happened?" John asked.

"I'm on it. I can dig around and see what kind of chatter is taking place in the darker corners of—"

"Parker, I have to call you back," John said, cutting Parker off.

* * *

John ended the call and looked around. He now noticed the unnerving scene around him. The people stopped talking. Everyone around him fixed their eyes to the nearest screens. Most were looking down at their phones, but John walked over to one of the news vans where the crew gathered around the monitors set up in the back.

As he got close, he saw a man seated at a table with a flag behind him. He recognized the Four Serpents emblem right away, but as he reached the van and heard the voice, his blood ran ice cold. Azhaar bin Hashim sat on the screen with a self-satisfied grin, addressing the world.

*"—but a small taste of our rage. You thought you had beheaded the serpent, but it is not that easy. We will not end our quest to teach the western world a lesson in pain and suffering.

"You send your oppressors, your barbarians to our gates to tear us from our homes, where we try to live our lives in peace. Those who would dare stick their hands into the serpent's lair shall suffer the venom of its strikes," bin Hashim said.

"Is this live?" John asked.

"I don't know," a woman holding the camera said. "It's a live broadcast, but I don't know if it's an actual live feed."

John grabbed her upper arm. "How can we find out? Is there a way to trace this back to the broadcast location?"

She just met his eyes with a near blank expression shaking her head before turning back to the monitor.

"The French government dared, and they have felt the fangs sink in deep. That was but a single bite." His face turning down, bin Hashim leaned into the camera. *"With the help of the Americans, you have dared to invade us. You are responsible for killing and kidnapping our families and friends."*

John stepped away, redialing Parker's number.

"Hey, John." Parker was distracted, the broadcast playing in the background.

"Kid, you have to find out where that transmission is coming from," John said.

Parker was quiet for a moment, his fingers clicking away at his keyboard.

"This broadcast is streaming live. I don't understand, is he a fake or—"

"It's him," John said. "We captured a double."

Parker sighed. *"What do we do now?"*

"Get me a location. I'm going to drag that snake from his hole and cut him to pieces."

CHAPTER
30

John and Curtis stepped out of the car, joining Gavreau and Silvestre as they walked into the Police Nationale offices. A pair of detectives joined them, shaking hands and offering condolences in French to the two RAID members. After a brief exchange, one of the men led them to a small conference room.

"He says they can offer us any aid in the hunt for the Four Serpents," Gavreau said. "Let us discuss our plan in here for now."

They gathered around the table as Silvestre set up a borrowed laptop, connecting it to the wall-mounted display. John dialed Parker's number on the teleconference system to pull him into the meeting.

"Hey John. Everyone."

"What have you got so far?" John asked.

"It would be much easier to show you," Parker said. *"Is there a computer there that I can link up with?"*

Silvestre looked over at Gavreau. "Lussier is the tech geek. I'm not sure how to—"

"Nevermind, I got it," Parker said. *"I need you to accept the request, though. No need to break in when one can get permission."*

The information from Silvestre's borrowed computer popped up on the screen.

"I thought you said it would be easier to show us," Curtis said. "We're looking at a list of numbers. Is that really what you wanted to show us?"

Parker typed away as more information popped up. *"Yes and no. This is the bad news portion of the presentation. These are all broadcast stations where the signal came from. It's widespread. Global."*

"Does that mean the Four Serpents are all over the world?" John asked.

"No, it doesn't appear so. These are all some type of remote relay stunt. They've got someone almost as good as I am. Almost," Parker said.

"Is there a point to all of this?" Gavreau asked.

"Uh, sorry, yes. The Four Serpents have some connections if they can accomplish this kind of broadcast."

"If they were able to pull this off in mere hours, we've got our hands full," Curtis said.

"The good news is, this very likely took weeks to pull off," Parker said. *"My guess is that this was how they had*

intended to let the world know of their first strike when they put Takada's research into play."

"And that is what happened," Silvestre said. "We were hit with those kinetic weapons."

Parker continued. *"Again, it's a good news, bad news situation. They hit your headquarters with the javelins, but they weren't able to use Takada's research to pull it off."*

"Well, their accuracy was astounding for not having the research," John said. "I hope the good news is helpful."

"Bin Hashim didn't have the long-strike capability that Takada's research would have given him. The drone violated French airspace to strike," Parker said. *"They scrambled a couple of Rafale fighter jets to take it down, but we've got enough data to trace it back to a general point of origin."*

"Well that's a start," John said. "How do we pinpoint their position?"

"That's where our friend Doctor Takada comes in. I reimaged his drives here and dug through the transmissions," Parker said.

Gavreau shot John a questioning glance.

"I know. I'm sorry. We will answer for all of this when it's done," John said.

"I don't care if he hacked the president's email, as long as he can point us to bin Hashim," Silvestre said.

"Anyway, I've got three sets of data, the broadcast hacks, the drone's flight path, and the IP addresses from Takada's

upload. Everything triangulates right here." Parker pulled up a map of a mountainous region, with a red circle drawn over it. *"Give or take a hundred yards."*

"Do you know where that is?" John asked.

Gavreau rested his elbows on the table, fists under his chin. "That is about one hundred and twenty miles southeast of here."

"We could have our team geared up and on the ground in an hour," Silvestre said. "Just get us on a chopper, sir."

John recognized the look in the RAID commander's eyes. He understood the urge to throw caution to the wind and leap into the fire, fueled by rage and a need for revenge. But there was a delicate balance between planning and speed that they would have to walk, to get the buy off they would need to acquire the support.

"How sure are you of the location, Parker?" John asked.

"I mean, you can never be one hundred percent, but if the Azhaar bin Hashim isn't holed up in those mountains, then they've got far more sophisticated resources," he said. *"And if that's the case, that means they've got backing from a superpower nation."*

"That's highly unlikely," John said. "Gavreau, you'll need to pull some resources from another

RAID unit, and the Police Nationale if we're going to stop the serpents."

"We?" Gavreau asked.

John met his steely gaze. "You're going to need all hands on deck. Curtis and I have the same level of experience and intel as you do. We can't risk going in with less than optimal fighting strength."

Gavreau brought a hand to his mouth thinking about John's words. "Perhaps you are correct. It will take some convincing, but I will pull some strings."

Curtis raised his hand. "Uh, I feel like maybe I should point out that I'm going to be pretty damn *suboptimal* in the field with a hole in my leg."

"You can provide support from the air," Silvestre said. "In the choppers."

* * *

"You will be joining us in the helicopters," Gavreau said to Curtis and John. "The other team will be mostly police and military support. This is all an off the books operation, with French and German military support on deck if things go badly for us."

"What's the plan, then?" Curtis asked.

John worked the bolt of the FN P90, ensuring the chamber was clear. "We're going to fast rope in, drop any opposition in our way, and defang the snake."

"And how will we know that this is the one and only Azhaar bin Hashim?" Silvestre asked.

John tapped his helmet, next to the camera. "Our man, Parker, will have access to the live feed during the operation. He'll have his computers overclocked and running full speed to process the data. His software will let us know if we see him."

"Does anyone know the layout of the base?" Curtis asked.

"We have minimal information," Gavreau said. "Once we are on the ground, you and the other door gunners will have to provide our close air support, targeting any significant threats, and suppressing the enemy.

"As much as we want bin Hashim, we need to remember that the real objective is to shut down the kinetic weapon system."

"Roger that," John said, tightening his gloves. "Parker will be monitoring any outgoing network transmissions during the op. We target the drone, and all of the computers they are using to control it. If anything gets out, he'll be able to zero in, and provide the location."

"Let's hope we're able to contain it," Curtis said. "We can't risk this information reaching someone else's hands."

"The blueprints for their drone have been distributed across all allied nations," Gavreau said. "We will at least be able to spot anything like it that any existing splinter groups can launch."

"For now, we should focus on our primary target. The head of the serpent," John said.

CHAPTER
31

The engines of the AS532 Cougar spooled up, the rotors slowly building the momentum they would need to lift the craft. John secured the P90 PDW to his body and chambered a round. He checked the HK USP 45, flipping the selector to safe before securing it into the drop leg holster.

Silvestre helped Curtis into one of the waiting helicopters, leaving the crutches behind as he settled in behind the 7.62mm machine gun mounted at the side door. Curtis gave him a nod, as Gavreau handed Silvestre his M4 carbine.

John shook hands with one of the men from the Police Nationale that helped equip him for the mission. He ducked and ran to the craft as the rotor wash whipped dirt and debris around. John adjusted his goggles and checked the fit of his helmet making sure the camera hadn't been knocked free.

"Can you hear me, John?" Parker asked.

"Loud and clear," he replied.

"Welcome to the team, Parker," Curtis said.

"I've got a semi-private channel with just the two of you, but I'll be doing the majority of my communicating across the four of you. I'll let Gavreau deal with the rest of the operation. My French doesn't extend much beyond fries and pizza."

"Neither of those is French," Curtis said.

"And that's why I'm going to defer to Gavreau when passing along the information."

"Ready?" Gavreau asked.

John, Curtis, and Silvestre all answered with a thumbs up, securing themselves into their seats.

The commander gave the signal to the pilot, and the Cougar lifted off. Two more AS532s rose shortly afterward. The three helicopters took off toward the serpent's hidden mountain base.

The chopping air from the rotors thrummed in John's chest as the craft skimmed along the ground before rising to a more stable elevation.

"I missed this," Curtis said. "Well, this part anyway. The shooting and getting shot at, not so much."

"Initial reports are showing that they believe the serpents base must be in a clearing at the foot of the mountain range, with some shallow tunnels running throughout the area," Gavreau said.

"Can we trust those reports?" John asked.

Gavreau pressed his lips together and shrugged. "It is probably safer to assume that they will be completely underground. That way we can just lob a few missiles and collapse the whole structure."

"Did we bring any missiles with us?" Curtis asked.

"No," Gavreau said. "My superiors did not like that suggestion."

"Our best play is to drop in far enough away to establish a solid fighting position," John said. "Let the choppers soften the opposition with the seven-six-twos."

"That I can do," Curtis said.

"We move up from there, careful not to let anyone escape, or flank us. Once inside, we stay tight in our fire teams," John said.

Gavreau nodded. "Everyone, stay in constant radio contact. We cannot risk losing sight of the objective. The kinetic weapon system must be destroyed."

"And Azhaar bin Hashim has to be stopped," John said.

"I will make sure of that, personally," Silvestre said, the fury in his eyes almost glowing.

John's harness dug into his shoulder as the helicopters all dipped lower, approaching the mountains.

"Five minutes," Gavreau said, pressing a finger to his ear.

"Five minutes," the rest of the occupants repeated.

* * *

The helicopters broke formation, each taking a separate path toward their objective. John gripped his harness as the pilot swung their craft in a full arc. Smoke streamed from the ground below as an RPG lanced into the sky, missing the chopper with the Police Nationale team onboard.

Smoke puffed from the side door as John watched the door gunner open up on the terrorist below. The rhythmic popping reached his ears a full second after he saw the pulsing muzzle flashes.

"I think they know we're here," Curtis said.

"They must have known we would be coming soon," Gavreau said.

"Is that good or bad?" Curtis looked at John for an answer.

"Focus on the mission, Lieutenant," John said.

Curtis nodded, his features straightened, set in stone.

"Right there," Gavreau said to the pilot pointing to a clearing, surrounded by trees and rocky outcropping.

The Cougar turned, *drifting* to the drop zone, covering the last dozen yards sideways.

"Go! Go! Go!" Gavreau shouted

Ropes fell from the bird on either side. John, Silvestre, Gavreau, and a member from another RAID unit slid down as the enemy fire sparked to life. The popping and whizzing of enemy fire let John know that they had some pretty stiff opposition.

John's boots hit the ground with a crunch. He held his weapon tight to his body and ran for the nearest rock for cover. Gavreau slid behind the boulder next to him as Silvestre, and the other man each found a tree.

The ropes wound up into the chopper as Curtis settled in behind his machine gun. The weapon thundered, and huge gouts of flame spit from the barrel. He worked the trigger in five-round bursts, putting rounds into a group of enemies until they were no longer a threat before pivoting to the next.

An RPG screamed by as the pilot reacted, wheeling the tail rotor out of the way. The maneuver swung Curtis out of position, no longer able to lay down his covering fire.

"They're in trouble up there," John shouted to the others. "We need to move up and press the attack."

Not waiting for the reply, John stepped out, P90 braced against his shoulder. He sighted toward the enemy and pressed the trigger, spitting a quick burst at the muzzle fire in the distance. Gavreau and the others followed suit, their M4s answering back.

John saw a pair of men crouching near a tree, one holding a launch tube while the other passed him a rocket-propelled grenade. He gritted his teeth and dropped to a crouch, pulling the weapon in tight as he fired three bursts. The armed man spun and fell, as the RPG streaked to the side, sending a group of serpents scrambling.

The enemy shifted their focus, turning the fire onto the men on the ground, assaulting their position. John slammed his shoulder into a tree, stopping his forward momentum as rifle fire tore up the dirt around him. The helicopter's rotors pulsed in the air, falling into a groove with Curtis' machine gun fire.

With the choppers pounding away at the forces on the ground, John and the others advanced again. The serpents that didn't retreat fell to the oncoming volume of fire from the troops storming the gates.

John squeezed another burst at team setting up a PKM. His shots cut the trigger man down just as his partner readied the weapon. A second burst dropped another serpent before they could get the machine gun into play.

John rushed ahead, as Gavreau and Silvestre drove another group of terrorists back.

"Curtis, the rocks and trees are going to cut off your line of sight, but if you can lay down a steady stream ahead of us, you'll clear the way for our entry," John said, cupping his hand over his mic to drown out the unyielding thunder roaring across the battlefield.

"Consider it done," he said.

Within seconds The AS532 Cougar roared overhead, engines rumbling and rotors pounding the ground. Curtis wheeled his to the side and charged his weapon, loading a fresh belt before unleashing hell. The streaks from his tracer rounds drew a bright, orange line of death across the enemy's ranks. John signaled to the others and advanced as the serpents hunkered down.

The other two choppers joined in as their gunners lit up the early evening sky. Tracers punched through the opposition, like lasers burning holes through paper. The serpents that survived the onslaught fell back into the base. John reached a boulder, mere yards from the front entrance of a building that appeared to be growing out of the rocky bottom of the mountain.

The choppers ceased their fire as the rest of the team reached their rally point. No longer able to provide an effective offense, the pilots pulled their helicopters away, switching to a flight pattern that would provide close air support and prevent reinforcements from flanking John and the others.

CHAPTER
32

"The enemy has fallen back," Gavreau said into his radio. "We must be careful with our advance from this point."

John nodded and looked at the building through his scope. It was rough in construction but appeared to be made out of reinforced concrete. It would have taken the enemy a long time to build this, all right under the French government's nose.

"How long has this base been here?" he asked.

Silvestre, Gavreau, and the final RAID assaulter just exchanged glances, shrugging.

"At least three months," Parker said. "Given the size of the structure. Of course, if that thing is connected to tunnels that burrow into the mountain, it would be even longer."

Gavreau scanned the area with his binoculars. "There is nowhere they would be able to launch or maintain a drone in that building. We must assume that they are inside the mountain. In a series of tunnels."

"Wonderful," John said, checking his weapon.

"If they have built that structure to repel an attack, they will cut us to ribbons while we cross that open field," Silvestre said.

John turned to look over his shoulder, and then back at the building ahead. "We should be able to get inside with minimal trouble."

"How can you be so sure?" Silvestre asked, fixing his red dot sight on the entrance.

"They built this here to hide," John said. "Yes, we're stuck in a bottleneck to cross that gap, but look over there."

He pointed to the front face of the structure.

"No firing ports. Only a few windows, set too high to effectively fight from," John said.

"So what are you suggesting?" Gavreau asked.

"If we put a high enough volume of fire on those windows, I can get to the door and press the attack. They'll have no choice but to fall back and let the rest of you come up."

"You have no idea what the inside of that building looks like," Gavreau said.

"The Cougars don't have rockets, and the machine guns would only chip away at the reinforced roof," John said. "Our best bet is to charge in there before they can dig in."

"I'm with John on this one," Curtis said. *"At least I would be, if I were down there with you guys."*

Silvestre shrugged, conceding the point.

"Alright," Gavreau said to John. "When I give the signal, we go."

Before John could protest, the commander had already started passing the instructions on to the rest of the teams in French. He twisted the ball off of his foot into the loose rocks and dirt, trying to find purchase to start his run when the RAID commander gave the signal.

Gavreau put a hand on John's shoulder and gave him two quick pats as he shouted the go signal to the rest of the teams. The muzzle flashes bloomed, flowers planted into the rocks, spitting projectiles at 2400 feet per second. John exhaled and pushed his body forward. Bullets smacked off the concrete facade and the windows shattered.

Enemy blooms sprouted from the base, answering back as several serpents fired blindly through the high windows. Puffs of dirt kicked rocks into John's body as he closed the distance. They were only ten meters from the front entrance when John adjusted his course to plant himself along the side, preparing to tell Gavreau that he would kick the door in.

The RAID commander reached the door right behind John. He shifted his grip on the M4, using the weapon mounted under the barrel of the carbine. John recognized it as a short-barreled Mossberg 500. Gavreau held the muzzle close to the door's latch and blasted a hole in the mild steel door. He racked the weapon and fired again, knocking a large chunk from the frame and sending the handle flying inward.

He pivoted and put his back to the wall as John immediately stepped into his role, falling back a step and planting a foot into the door. The metal slab swung inward violently, the thundering clang echoing down the hall as John and Gavreau stepped inside.

The entryway ended at a short T-intersection. John signaled for Gavreau to cover the right, as he leaned out along the left. The path opened up to a broader walkway, windows on the left and a pair of doors on the right. The men inside were still attempting to stand on boxes and chairs to return fire.

Kneeling and using the wall for cover, John shouldered his P90 and punched a trio of holes in the back of one the serpents. Gavreau's carbine rattled the walls along the other side as he barked commands in the radio for the others to advance.

A pair of men whirled around and opened up with their AKs, aiming too high. John held his ground and put the front sight on the first, pressing the trigger before swinging the muzzle to the right and dumping the rest of the magazine into the man. The PDW spit a dozen 5.7mm projectiles into his target's body in less than a second.

The last serpent let out a cry and whipped his weapon around. John's hand fell to the USP 45 as he drew the handgun and pressed it forward. He strode around the corner and placed four rounds center mass, sending the man crashing to the floor.a

Echoes of the last of the shots still reverberated through the concrete halls as John walked forward, pistol in his hands. "Clear."

"Clear," Gavreau answered back.

Silvestre stepped through, followed by the other RAID man, limping from a wound in his leg. The police came in afterward as they all assembled in one of the wider passages. John holstered the 45 and swapped mags in his P90.

"How do we proceed?" Silvestre asked.

John looked at the wounded man with Silvestre. "You two stay here and hold this corridor. There are two doors on each side, so we should check them out in pairs, all at the same time."

Gavreau translated, and the rest of the men acknowledged. John and the RAID commander stacked up on the far door in the left passageway. As the other teams entered their doors, John eased his open, keeping his weapon close to his body, turning at the waist to sweep his muzzle across the dark hall.

"It's a tunnel," he said.

Gavreau stepped past John, flicking his weapon light on. "Looks like they are all inside."

John clicked his light on and nodded at the commander as he took point. Shortly after entering, the top of the tunnel sloped down, almost brushing against their helmets. Both men hunched as they moved forward. Their beams swept side to side when John noticed a deeper shadow along the right side.

"There's a path that branches off," he said.

With his weapon up, John advanced one step at a time, drifting to the left to take the corner in slices. A shadow flickered across his view.

"Tango!" he shouted, pushing Gavreau against the wall as he pinned himself against the other side.

A man turned the corner and ran straight ahead, shooting his rifle blindly behind him. Bullets tossed chunks of stone at them. They advanced, firing as the muzzle flashes and bouncing light beams obscured their target.

At the branching path, another man lunged from the shadows. John had his weapon up in time to deflect the blade thrusting at his chest. He twisted his body and whipped an elbow across the man's jaw, sending him sprawling ahead in the tunnel. John rushed forward as the serpent rose to his feet.

A metallic thunk rang out as something wobbled along the ground past John. "Grenade!"

He grabbed the man's collar and spun him around, putting him between himself and the explosive, as he backpedaled. Gavreau darted into the branching path, getting clear of the weapon's blast radius as it detonated. The air shook, hitting John in the chest like a battering ram. His human shield fell on him as they hit the ground.

Deep rumbling and cracking rocked the tunnel. A chunk of the ceiling broke free, falling near John. He kicked the dead man's body off and crawled away as more rubble dropped down, blocking the passage. Footsteps echoed as he rolled onto his stomach, punching a trio of holes in the back of the man that threw the grenade.

"Gavreau, are you ok?" he asked, pushing himself up to a crouch to cover the tunnel.

"Gavreau?" John stood and put a hand on the wall of rocks blocking his way back. "Parker, can you reach Gavreau?" he tapped the mic. "Curtis? Anyone?"

Just great, he thought. *The mountain is blocking the radio signals.*

* * *

John switched to several different frequencies, trying to reach the team. He set his radio back to the original channel and took a deep breath, exhaling through flared nostrils.

John switched the weapon light off, letting his eyes adjust to the darkness. A faint glow from the far end slowly revealed the details of the textured walls as his pupils dilated. He eased ahead, careful with the placement of his feet with each step. At another branch, he stepped slowly around the corner until he could see a large hollow, this one unoccupied.

He nudged the crate on the floor along the back wall, looking at the flares inside. He took a couple and stuffed them into a pouch on his left thigh. *Could come in handy.*

At the end of the tunnel, the path curved to the left. Only this time, instead of the rough cut tunnels he emerged from, this was more sophisticated, with lighting fixtures every 10 to 12 yards, casting a yellow glow from each. Someone had set up sturdy supports, and the ceiling rose to a slightly more comfortable 7 feet high.

John rechecked the radio signal. "Parker? Gavreau?"

The tunnel shifted directions again, curving ahead. John noticed the lighting fixtures had a tendency to wipe his shadow across the walls ahead as he walked. He moved only several feet at a time before crouching and leaning his body slowly to give himself a better mental image of what he was walking into.

The rounded end of a shadow poked out across the floor before receding again. Echoing footsteps followed close behind. John pressed his body against the wall and slid along, easing around the supports as he traversed the bend in the tunnel.

John used the support at one of the lighting fixtures for cover. The light would illuminate him if anyone looked carefully, but it wouldn't throw his shadow forward, giving away his position just yet. The figure returned, walking to a stack of crates as it lifted one up and walked away again. John fished the monocular from one of the pockets in his vest and leaned out for a better view.

He lowered the monocular, confused for a moment before raising it up again. The tunnel ended about a quarter of a mile ahead, expanding to an expansive space. *How long have they been building this?* he thought.

This was not the type of facility he had expected the Four Serpents to have constructed. What John saw would have required far more resources than they had expected. In the opened space, he saw a pair of temporary buildings, like the kind used on construction sites, set up end to end.

"What are you up to, bin Hashim?"

John tucked the monocular back into his vest and raised his P90, pulling it into his shoulder as he walked ahead. The man returned to the stack of crates. John crouched in place, hoping to minimize his shadow, disguising its silhouette. The man hoisted the box and walked away, John hurried, making it to the open space.

The muzzle of his weapon following his gaze, John reached the first temporary office. His boots rang softly on the diamond plate steel steps as he approached the door. John put his ear against the wood, listening inside. He spotted the crate mover returning, and eased the door open, slipping inside before someone spotted him.

The buzz of fluorescent lights and faux wood paneled walls almost made John forget that he was in the heart of a mountain. He approached a desk, rifling through some of the papers in neat stacks.

"Shipping manifests?" John raised an eyebrow, folding one of the pages up and slipping it into his back pocket.

A faint voice echoed in the distance. Someone shouting in Arabic. More voices joined in, answering or acknowledging what the first man said. Serpents on alert and rushing to battle stations. John crouched underneath the window in the trailer as the group moved away. Looks like the others were putting up a good fight.

Another page caught John's eye as he shifted some of the sheets to the side, revealing blueprints for a drone. He only had a second to look at the page when the stairs at the front clanged and rattled. John. Brought his weapon up just as the door swung open. The crate man stared at the stranger in his trailer, his hand snapping to the grip of his rifle.

John's PDW split the air, stitching five rounds in a jagged line up the man's torso, the last bullet cracking his collarbone. The man staggered backward, tumbling down the stairs as his AK chattered. *Well if they didn't hear my shots, they undoubtedly would have heard that.*

As if on cue, shouting and thumping steps rushed toward the trailers. The back door flew open as an overweight man barged in. John whirled around and dropped to a crouch, pumping the man's body with bullets. As his body fell forward, another man was already storming in, rifle barking. John drove his body to the side, shoulder slamming into the wall and rocking the trailer.

He returned fire, sending two long bursts at the serpent, leading his target as he attempted to dodge. John's weapon ran dry as a third terrorist barged in, his shotgun releasing a thunderclap in the close quarters.

John pivoted behind a steel filing cabinet, letting his weapon fall to its sling and hoisting the heavy office furniture up. The shotgun exploded again, but the cabinet absorbed much of the buckshot as John charged ahead. He slammed into the serpent, the weight of the steel filing cabinet adding to the force of the impact.

The terrorist winced in pain as the collision cracked several of his ribs. John hurled the filing cabinet out the door, sending two more men diving to the side to avoid being crushed. John wrapped an arm around his foe's head and wrenched it to his right. As the terrorist's body slumped to the floor, John caught the shotgun before it hit the ground.

He stepped out the back door, twirled the firearm around, and unleashed another fusillade of lead shot, exploding another man's chest. John racked the weapon and blasted the second serpent, shredding his shoulder and severing the arm. The pump let out another *ka-chock* as John finished the screaming man's misery.

His boots rang out as he went down the steps, heading for the second trailer. The door opened, and John brought the shotgun up. The man coming out looked down the barrel, eyes wide, struggling to hold his Skorpion steady.

Both men squeezed the trigger at the same time, the serpent's bullets flying over John's head, into the first trailer as the double-aught buckshot slammed into his foe's chest, hurling him back into the next temporary office.

John bounded up the steps and stepped over the body, racking the weapon again. As he passed the entryway, a blur of movement closed in, a glint of steel leading the way. Bringing the shotgun up, John blocked the machete as it clanged off the steel body. He deflected the attack and swung the barrel back, pressing the trigger. *Click*

The madman swiped with the blade again as John leaned back, barely escaping the killing blow. He slammed the stock of the shotgun into the man's jaw, cracking the bone and sending the serpent flying out the window.

John saw one more man in the office with him, and whipped the shotgun through the air, in a flat spin like a boomerang. The barrel struck the terrorist's face, exploding in a spray of blood, saliva, and teeth. Drawing the USP, he ended the man's misery with a double tap, sending a pair of .45 caliber slugs through him.

The firefight now over, voices from further in the caves echoed as they approached. John scanned the immediate area with his pistol before swapping the partial mag for a full one and sliding the weapon into its holster. He picked up the AK-47 from the last man and stepped over his body, exiting the office.

I guess they know I'm here now, he thought. John checked the selector, finding it still set to fire, and exited the second office trailer, making his way ahead, into the dark tunnels ahead.

CHAPTER
33

The large space narrowed again branching off into a series of tunnels. John could hear voices, almost arguing. He turned his head and listened. Distant popping and thumps let him know Gavreau and the others were still in the fight.

Something dripped onto his earlobe. He wiped it away and glanced down at the blood on his gloved fingertips. John dabbed at his ear, taking note at the stinging pain. His adrenaline was receding and no longer working to mask the smaller wounds across his body.

Buckshot, grenade shrapnel, and flying shards of glass had all done a number, slicing small lines and punching tiny holes in various limbs. John couldn't help but smile. With everything the enemy had thrown at him, including the kinetic-strike javelins, he could only count himself as lucky.

"Can't get lazy now, John," he said, swinging the rifle's sling over his body and heading into the dark network of tunnels.

* * *

Pausing to let his eyes adjust again, John crept forward. The discussions in the deeper tunnels separated, and he could tell now that only three men approached, judging by their conversations. They spoke in a mix of French and Arabic, but John still had no idea what they were saying.

He spotted another hollow in the wall and sliced the corner before settling inside. This one was deeper than the other two, starting to turn before ending. He bent down at the box along the back wall, lifting the lid. *Flares. Again.*

It wasn't clear what the serpents were doing with the branches, but John could only guess that these were expansions or additional paths to the larger clearings. Before he made it back to the central tunnel, the flickering glow and hiss of a flare clattered along the ground up ahead.

The angry red glow exposed another hollow up ahead on the other side of the tunnel. John held the front sight of the rifle, expecting someone to emerge, but instead, a figure rounded the bend of the primary pathway.

The man wore a suit much different than the other serpents John had faced up to this point. More tactical in nature, with hard shell knee and elbow pads, and a helmet. The man had a bullpup weapon of some type, close to his body. Perfect for fighting in tight spaces like a network of tunnels. *Perfect,* John thought.

Another figure followed behind, and a third, with the same loadout as the first man. As they approached the hollow up ahead, the serpent in the lead shifted his angle to cover anyone that may have been hiding in there while the other two kept their aim straight ahead.

He wouldn't be able to stay hidden while they pass. Even with the short bend in his side passage. John had no other choice but to engage, while he had a half decent fighting position. He held the front sight on one of the men in the back, aiming his way. John tucked his elbows in, braced his rifle and let out a slow breath as he pressed the trigger.

Chaos erupted from the muzzle as the flash pulsed in the darkness. As the light faded, John saw the man stagger away in the flare's light. The other two spun and opened up on his position.

The report from their rifles came in precise, three-round bursts, the muzzle flashes constrained to the sides, like the wings of a phoenix. Bullets carved gouges and knocked dents into the stone walls.

John dropped to a crouch and leaned out again, opening up. His shots hit the wall in the distance as the lead serpent ducked into the hollow. The second man had also crouched, pressing his body against the wall. The third man rose to his feet again.

Body armor. He cursed and opened fire once more, rewarded with a puff on the chest of the serpent, knocking him down again.

"Stay down, this time," he shouted.

John knew the man was still in the fight, but getting hit in the chest with a sledgehammer, even in body armor had a demotivating effect that he hoped would sap some of the motivation out of the man.

The other two returned fire, a series of tight bursts lighting up the tunnels. John took cover again. He could hear the men talking. If he had to guess, they were planning to rush his position.

No doubt the third man surviving multiple hits only served to confirm the effectiveness of their armor. He leaned out and fired another pair of bursts. The serpents answered as all three men carved away at the wall.

The leader shouted something, and the shooting stopped. Rocks and pebbles falling and bouncing along the tunnel surfaces blended with the approaching boot steps, gravel crunching as the serpents slithered forward.

John cradled the AK in his arms and retrieved one of the flares from his pocket, pulling the cap. "I surrender. Please, don't kill me."

"Come out. Hands up, American," one of the serpents snapped.

Snapping the striker across the tip, the flare hissed to life. He leaned out and tossed it at the lead terrorist. The second man hadn't come as far, and the third took cover in the distant hollow.

The flare's glow flipped, end over end, playing tricks with the shadows. The serpent knocked the light to the side with his weapon, sending a shower of sparks as it struck. John had the AK against his body as he stepped out fully, advancing as the rifle roared to life, shaking more debris loose.

The heavy slugs didn't penetrate his foe's body armor, but a half dozen jackhammer blows to the sternum had its own distinct flavor that John could use to his advantage when cooking up chaos.

Dropping the now empty AK, he grabbed hold of the lead man's weapon, using it spin him around and pin their bodies together. The second serpent raised his rifle, but hesitated, not wanting to kill his own man.

That falter cost him as John drew his pistol and raised it up, squeezing off three shots. The first round cracked the lens of the goggles in a blood-spattered spiderweb. The next two rounds sparked off his helmet as the serpent crumbled.

The third man leaned out, ready to fire. John, hoping for more luck, shifted his aim. Before he could press the trigger, his hostage struck his wrist with a hammer fist, knocking the USP 45 from his grip. John tried to grab hold of the man's free hand when the serpent drove his helmeted head back into John's face.

He heard a crunch and felt a wet spray splash over his mouth and chin. A bright flash pulsed in his head as his eyes watered. John blinked away the pain as the terrorist spun around. Before he could fire, John forced the barrel down and away with one hand and pushed forward, launching a powerful elbow across his foe's face, returning the kindness.

The serpent fell, tugging at the weapon in John's other hand. He maintained his grip, reaching down with the other hand to wrap around the rifle. He watched the third terrorist emerge from the hollow with his weapon raised. John hoisted the injured serpent up by the weapon's sling as he brought the front sight up.

Both men fired. John held his ground, ready and steady as his foe leaped to the side, sending his shots wide. John tracked his movements and sent another two bursts, stitching holes through his target's body. To John's relief, the rifle's rounds penetrated the armor, dropping the serpent for good.

The leader reached up to wrench the weapon free of John's grasp, but he brought a boot down, stomping the man's head into the ground and tearing the clasp from the sling, freeing the rifle. He triggered a final burst to finish the man and tore the other end of the sling free from the fore end.

He ejected the empty magazine and found another on the man's body, glancing down at the odd appearance. *Caseless ammunition.*

"This is a little sophisticated for some snakes hiding in a mountain," he said, reloading the rifle.

CHAPTER
34

Following the trail of flares, John clutched the rifle close to his body, leaning to the side as he rounded the corner. Like before, this tunnel also opened up, but this time when he reached an area where he could stand comfortably, the path ended in a steel door.

Checking the handle and finding it unlocked, John stepped into the entrance, keeping his weapon trained ahead. He eased the door closed, letting it latch when he noticed a strange crackling and popping.

He knelt on one side of the hall and put a finger to his ear, keeping his voice low.

"Parker? Is that you?"

He could make out what sounded like a transmission, broken up into small pieces, only syllables slipping through the static. John looked around as he walked to the end of the short entryway, like an airlock.

A second door greeted him, this time with a tall and narrow window along the upper right corner. The glass had reinforcing wires crisscrossing diagonally.

The room on the other side was massive compared to the first area with the trailers. The window allowed him to see how high the ceiling went, looking more like a natural cave about twenty feet high. But it wasn't wide enough for John to see very far on either side.

Like the first door, this one was also unlocked. John had to push against the door with his shoulder, fighting the pressure from the other side. He slipped by the narrow gap, not wanting to open the door any further, and eased it shut.

John stepped further inside and found a deep shadow along one of the walls, and knelt down in it to stay hidden.

"—*opy? I repeat, this is Parker, do you copy?*"

"Parker. Good to hear your voice again," he said.

"*Is the rest of the team ok?*" Parker asked.

John turned his head to one side, listening for the distant battles still raging on. "I think so. The serpents have their hands full fighting against someone."

"*Where are you guys? Is Gavreau there?*"

"We were separated. I pushed ahead and ended up in a giant cave." John looked around, finally noticing a couple of men working to move some parts from one area, full of opened crates, to the far end.

"*I can see your feed again,*" Parker said. "*What are all those cables for?*"

John scanned the floor, spotting the large bundles snaking along the ground, into a side tunnel. Unlike the other passages, a bright light cast its glow from the depths, brighter than where he was.

"Give me a minute. I'll find out," he said.

John stood up just enough to see over some equipment where the cables disappeared into the darkness in the distance. He saw a faint bluish flickering glow on the far end of the area.

"I think it's computer equipment," John said. "This could be our primary objective."

"*Fantastic. John, You have to make sure nothing makes it out of there. No flash drives, no floppy discs, nothing.*" Parker stressed the importance of the mission through his tone, none of the usual jovial nature left.

"You can count on it," John said.

He made his way along one of the curving walls, toward the point of origin of the bundled cables. As he moved deeper into the cave, his eyes pulled more details from everything inside, aided by a semi-circle of work lights.

"*Is that a truck?*" Parker asked.

259

"Yeah. Looks like a fuel tanker," John said. "The only way they could get that in here is if that tunnel with the cables heads outside."

"That's got to be it," Parker said. *"It explains why you've got a signal again."*

John raised his weapon, sighting down the barrel as he stepped further into the cave. He kept his focus on the fuel tanker parked close to the center of the massive cavern.

Reaching the cable bundle, John turned to peer down the tunnel, seeing a series of work lights, like the ones set up inside. In the distance, he could see trees and a sliver of the night sky.

"This tunnel leads outside," he said. "I don't see anyone there. They must all be inside working."

Pivoting to follow the cables to the equipment inside, John moved quicker, stopping next to the truck as he heard some more voices. He saw two younger men in the distance grabbing more parts, but someone else was yelling something at them.

On the other side, he spotted part of a drone. The fuselage was mostly assembled, but the wings were sitting on a separate rack.

"Probably won't fit through the tunnel if they left the wings on," Parker said, finishing John's thoughts.

John swept the area, looking for the man shouting at the young serpents. He found a large muscular man and put the rifle sights on him. The man wore an outfit similar to the three he just fought in the central tunnel.

John saw a rifle, like the one he held, strapped to his back. He broke clear of the truck and ran in a low crouch next to the rack with the wings.

He moved again, making his way next to a cart with various tools and bundles of wires, kneeling to stay out of sight. The whine of an electric motor announced the arrival of an offroad vehicle of some sort.

A second man, just as big as the first, and dressed the same, stepped out and walked into the glow of the work lights. John froze, watching the leader step out and walk quickly to the computers. He turned and pointed around, barking more commands.

For another minuted John watched the man walking around, hurriedly making preparations at the drone.

"I'm sure your gut is telling you the same thing my software is. That's Azhaar bin Hashim."

"This ends here," John said.

"Look, I know what you're going to say, but don't you think you should wait for the others?" Parker asked.

"You and I both know that there's no way to let them know what I see here."

261

"Wait. I'm going to patch Curtis in on this conversation. Maybe he can have the pilot swing the chopper around the mountain to find that tunnel," Parker said, almost pleading.

"There's no time. It looks like he's downloading the data to a portable drive," John said. "I need to shut that computer down, and stop bin Hashim here."

* * *

He stepped out as one of the bodyguards spun around. Before John could put his sights on bin Hashim, the big man stepped into the path of the incoming burst.

The rounds thumped him in the gut, piercing the armor. The serpent dropped to his knees, but he reached back to bring his rifle into the fight.

John cursed and bolted as the second man had his weapon up, snapping out several bursts. John dove and rolled behind a crate with spare parts for the drone.

He rose up fast, catching the enemy off guard, and fired at the first guard again, killing him. The serpent fell back, arm out to the side as his weapon spit a three round burst, killing one of the younger men assembling the drone.

The second bodyguard advanced, firing a series of bursts, the penetrator rounds punching holes through John's cover. He stayed low, moving to the side to find another barrier. A bullet slipped through the crate, lancing through John's left upper arm.

He felt the heat and pain pulse out, but the next burst stopped cold as John pressed his back against a heavy rack, full of metallic cylinders, tapering to a point. The bodyguard fired again, the bullets bouncing off the tungsten-rich rods John used for protection.

His left arm weak and shaking, John used his good arm to prop himself up against the rack and return fire. The foolish serpent had been standing out in the open, advancing on his prey.

John's rifle spit burst after burst, perforating the serpent's chest and head. His weapon clicked empty. John stood, looking for bin Hashim as his hand fell to the drop leg holster. *Nothing.* The pistol had been knocked from his grip in an earlier confrontation.

The head of the serpents let out a cry of fury and opened fire with the first dead bodyguard's rifle. John dove forward and rolled behind a series of stalagmites. Azhaar bin Hashim circled the rocks, probing out with repeated bursts.

"It is too late, Stone!" he shouted, his voice echoing in the cave.

"It's not too late," John said. "Surrender now. Maybe I'll just break your arms and leave your legs alone."

"You Americans are all the same. You think the battle is never lost as long as you still have your tongue to spit out clever little quips," bin Hashim said.

"I was basing that on the fact that you're surrounded, most of your men are dead, and I'm in a pretty bad mood," John said.

The serpent rocked his head back, bellowing in laughter. "Once I kill you, I will escape, and the *God Hand* will still be in my possession. The western world will never be able to stop the Four Serpents, as we encircle the globe."

Azhaar bin Hashim stepped quickly to the side, bringing the rifle up just as he reached a position giving him a clear line of sight. But John was listening to the sound of his voice and tracking bin Hashim's movement, waiting for his moment to strike.

The Serpent leader's muzzle sparked, spitting out wings of flames to either side. John had already changed directions, charging back to the drone parts.

He skidded to a stop, grabbing one of the javelins off the rack. Bin Hashim swung the muzzle to track the Ranger. He pressed the trigger, unleashing full-auto fury.

Hoisting the dense, kinetic-strike javelin to his shoulder, John stepped forward, driving his full weight into the throw. A bullet punched through John, just below his ribs, as he hurled the tapered rod, letting out a grunt through clenched teeth.

The impact sent a jarring wave through his body. He dropped to a knee, catching himself with his uninjured arm. The kinetic javelin slammed into Azhaar bin Hashim, driving him backward. His body struck a tanker truck behind him, and a loud ring reverberated through the cavern.

John rose to his feet, steadying himself on the crates of spare parts. The rifle fell from bin Hashim's hand, clattering to the floor. He clutched the tungsten rod protruding from his chest and coughed gouts of blood. The javelin had punched through his body, separating ribs as it passed through, just below his heart. His body was slack, but stayed upright, pinned to the truck.

Jet fuel and blood poured from the wound, pooling at bin Hashim's feet. A trail of the reddish fluid snaked outward.

His lung was punctured, and his life poured out in dark red pulsing streams. Wheezing his last breaths, bin Hashim glared at his enemy with fiery hatred. John watched the strength seep from the man through squinted eyes.

He limped forward, pulling the last flare from the pouch on his thigh. Popping the cap to expose the tip, he looked the leader of the Four Serpents in the eye.

"You should lighten up," John said and sparked the stick to life

He tossed the hissing flare on the ground, in the oncoming path of bloody fuel.

The liquid reached the flare, birthing a serpent of intense flame. The fire flashed toward the dying man, engulfing his entire body in a *whoosh*. Rasping hisses escaped the man's lips as he writhed in agony.

John rushed across the open cavern, toward the exit tunnel on the other side. The sound of the explosion dominated his senses. The solid rock walls shook and crumbled, as a wave of heat washed over his body.

The flames swirled around inside the cave, following him into the tunnels. John pistons his legs, and dove around a corner. Fire splashed off the walls all around him before the intense burning heat finally subsided.

John groaned as he stood, casually patting a small flame off his pant leg. He used the loops and clasps on his vest to support his left arm and clutched a hand over the wound in his side. John continued through the tunnel, until he emerged on the other side of the mountain, and headed for the tree line in the distance.

"What about the computers? The Drone?" Parker asked.

John felt the rumble, deep in the mountain's heart. Popping and crackling rattled the air. He looked over his shoulder as he stepped out into the fresh night air. "That's all taken care of."

John made sure Parker had a clear view through the tactical cam of the cave collapsing, crushing the God Hand underneath a literal mountain of rock. The tunnel followed shortly after. John raised an arm to shield his face from the dust cloud that belched out.

"Whoa," Parker said, drawing the word out. *"Is that it? Did we win?"*

"Yeah, kid. We won."

CHAPTER
35

"I see you," Curtis said.

John waved at the chopper, as he walked to a clearing in the trees, where the pilot would be able to land.

"Have you reached the others yet?" John asked.

"One of the police guys reached an area with a better signal," Parker said. *"I struggled for a bit with an online translator, but then Gavreau came back out, and I let him know what had happened."*

"Did anyone get hurt in the collapse?"

"No, Gavreau and Silvestre were able to reach the other teams and pull them back. I imagine feeling the mountain around you shaking had to be pretty unnerving," Parker said.

"You have got that right," Gavreau said, joining in on the conversation. *"Please do me a favor. If I ever say something crazy, like suggesting to bring you on another operation, slap some sense into me."*

"That I can do," John said.

* * *

The AS532 Cougar sat in a clearing, in front of the remains of the Four Serpents' hidden base. Inside the helicopter, a medic bandaged John's arm and worked to stop the bleeding in his torso.

"Are you sure, you do not want any painkillers?" the man asked in a heavy accent.

"Ask me again once we're sure the mission is over," John said.

Gavreau checked on his men, as another medic tended to other injuries. He shook hands with everyone nearby and tucked his helmet under an arm before walking over to John.

"You are sure that it was Azhaar bin Hashim in there?" he asked, pointing a thumb over his shoulder.

"My gut says so," John said. "But since I know you're more of an evidence guy, Parker's mob recognition software places the probability at about ninety-nine percent."

"Good enough for me." Gavreau pulled his gloves off, tucked them into his helmet, and tossed it into the chopper.

"Is that it, then?" John asked.

Gavreau looked up toward the peak of the mountain with a sigh. "Dr. Takada is dead. Azhaar bin Hashim and all of Takada's research is buried under that." He looked John in the eye. "But we can never be too sure."

John nodded, agreeing with the sentiment.

"Thank you, my friend." Gavreau extended a hand.

With a firm grasp, the two men exchanged nods and mutual respect for one another. John watched him as he rejoined the others. Curtis limped over and climbed into the Cougar with a grunt.

"So, bin Hashim is twice dead," he said. "What next? Hunt down his pets?"

John smiled and pressed a hand on the bandage over the wound through is triceps. "If his dog learns to pilot a drone, then Fido is on the list."

Epilogue

"Kind of like in the movies, overcast skies at a time like this, isn't it?" Parker asked.

John didn't answer, only looking down from the top of a hill at the large crowd gathered below. Word of Marvin Van Pierce's death spread fast through the network and other government agencies. The sea of people below had turned out for the man's funeral. Full military honors.

John and Parker watched the ceremony from a distance, and Curtis joined shortly after, leaning on a cane. Dr. Miranda Spencer held his other hand, helping him climb the hill. She gave the others a small, sad smile.

"He had some career," Curtis said, leaning on the cane with both hands.

"I would consider my life a huge success if I had half that turnout at my funeral," Parker said. "A quarter, even."

Still stoic, John just watched as the honor guard folded and presented the flag to a woman off to the side. He didn't recognize her, having almost no exposure to Van Pierce's personal life. John knew virtually nothing of the man outside of the work they had done together.

Riflemen lined up, firing volley shots on command, saluting the man that they had come to honor. After a while, everything ended, and the crowd thinned. John just stood, still as an oak, watching and waiting.

Curtis put a hand on his shoulder. "Marvin was a great man. This is a huge loss for the world."

"How many lives did he save?" John asked. He looked at Curtis. "How many more are in danger without a man like that doing what he did every day?"

"I'm not so sure it can be measured that easily," Curtis said. "People like that don't come along too often."

"It's up to us to fill that void," John said.

"What do you mean?" Miranda asked.

"You're not talking about joining another government team, are you?" Parker looked at the others in turn, a mix of confusion and concern twisting his features.

"No. I'm not just talking about us," John said.

"This world has grown complacent," Curtis said. "Apathetic to the battles happening around them, everywhere. Every day."

"Then society has to start small," John said. "But when men like Azhaar bin Hashim or the Four Serpents rise up, we've got to strike back. Together."

"Right," Parker said. "It's a team effort."

"And we'll be there to answer the call," Curtis said. "For MVP."

John looked at Curtis, the corner of his mouth turning up in a hint of a smile. "Like you said, it's not every day the world has someone like that watching over them."

DID YOU LIKE THIS BOOK?

Let us know by leaving a review. It only takes a moment and helps us, and independent authors, tremendously.

In our schedule of books, we have a ton of different ideas we would like to work on, but if you loved reading about John Stone, and want us to continue to tell his story, you, as the reader, can let us know directly. It is very difficult for us to get an idea of which books work without that feedback.

Let others know about it as well, and encourage them to leave a review. Right now, our future releases are all based on reader feedback, so if we don't know you liked the book, future sequels will sit in the queue along with the rest.

Thank you in advance!
The Manning Brothers

More from The Manning Brothers:

Nine Millie: Execution Style
Chance Hunter: Hunter Killer
Ty Octane: Terminal Velocity
Miami Winter: A Scott Maverick Thriller

Also Available from the Manning Brothers
Superhero action and adventure!
Two Percent Power: Delivering Justice
Spilled Milk: Two Percent Power Book 2

Thank you for reading!

If you liked this story, and would like to find out about more, join the Manning Brothers reader group and stay up to date on the progress of ALL of our future books. You will receive a link to download FREE stories, as well as notifications keeping you up to date on all new releases. You'll also receive special offers, intended only for subscribers.

www.EvilTwinBrian.com/join

About the Manning Brothers

Raised on a steady diet of action movies, professional wrestling, and comic books, We grew up in the 80s, believing ninjas were everywhere, and having a cool car was part of being a hero. The muscular man-of-action was the prototypical image of the person you expected to save the day. Over the years, that has changed, only serving to broaden the offering, giving us awesome protagonists of all types (including robots! Johnny Five is Alive!!).

It is this chapter in our lives that the Tag Team Champs were born. Allen had an idea: Bring the archetype of the unstoppable force of justice from our favorite action movies of the 1980s, set in today's world. John Rambo, John Matrix. John McClane...John Stone. The Hard

Kill was the first book we had planned to write, but then Brian had a crazy plan as well: Write a book with heroes inspired by movies from other decades a well.

In Hunter Killer, Chance Hunter, a Detroit homicide detective, brought the high-kicking martial arts heavy flavor of the 90s. Terminal Velocity's Ty Octane pushed action to the limit, inspired by the fast and furious movies in the new millennium. In Execution Style, Nine Millie fought with a gritty, realism portrayed in modern-day action flicks.

What's next you ask? We've toyed around with a couple of crossovers in our previous books, but the John Stone series will see all of our characters come together in one shared world, tackling a rogues gallery of threats that pose a real danger to everyone! They must all join forces, forming the Hard Core, to save the world from a global threat.

We have taken our love of action movies and turned it into a desire to tell stories that entertain other fans of the same flicks. Muscles, mustaches, and mayhem! We love writing books full of flying fists, car chases, big fireball explosions, and non-stop action. If that's what you're looking for, then welcome to the fold.

Made in the USA
Las Vegas, NV
19 December 2021

38910532R00163